The Crystal and The Cloud

She was a sickly, illiterate child, living in an obscure French slum in the middle of the nineteenth century. No-one guessed that when she went to gather drift-wood from the riverside she had taken the first steps on a journey leading to canonisation and to the establishment of one of the greatest pilgrim centres in the world. The child was Bernadette Soubirous, the town Lourdes, and on the banks of the river she met Aquero, the strange, radiant being whom only she could see.

This book tells of these meetings, of the events that followed them, and of the people whose lives were changed by them, from Louise who feared her daughter's powers to L'Abbé Peyramale who tried to discover the truth. Above all it is the story of Bernadette, the little girl who said, 'I am stupid but I know how to love', and of her intimate friendship with someone beyond human understanding.

Maureen Peters

The Crystal
and The Cloud

ROBERT HALE · LONDON

© *Maureen Peters 1977*

First published in Great Britain 1977

ISBN 0 7091 6170 0

Robert Hale Limited
Clerkenwell House
Clerkenwell Green
London EC1R 0HT

Printed in Great Britain by
Clarke, Doble & Brendon Ltd,
Plymouth and London

When it was too cold and windy to sit still, the child walked briskly up and down the twisting path with Pigou, the dog, bounding at her heels. The sheep were huddled in the big wooden barn that clung to a patch of level ground below the snow-capped peaks. Many lambs had been born that year, which meant an increased profit for Monsieur Lagues, and more good humour from Madame Lagues who was apt to be irritable when times were hard. Certainly it was more peaceful up on the hillside than in the bustling family home where nobody stopped talking to listen to anybody else. There were times when her head ached with trying to weave the strands of conversation into a coherent whole.

Today the wind had dropped and a fine, damp mist swirled up from the valley. If she strained her eyes it was almost possible to believe that she could see the roof of Le Cachot and the lights that burned in the windows of the bigger houses where the gentry lived. Her mother took in washing for a lady who lived in such a house, and on washing day there was a good mutton bone to enrich the cabbage-stew, and some pancakes if there were eggs to spare.

Two figures, solid black shadows in the fading light, were plodding towards her. She knew the one well, for he was her godmother's brother and parish priest of the tiny village of Bartres. The other she knew by sight as the schoolmaster, but as she did not attend school she had never spoken to him.

Now both the gentlemen paused as she bobbed a curtsey and stood aside to let them pass.

"The mist is rising. You ought to be driving down the sheep, child," Monsieur Aravant scolded.

"I'm nearly on my way, Monsieur le Curé," she said promptly.

"Is this the Soubirous girl?" enquired Monsieur Barbet, staring at the diminutive figure with a faint scowl.

"My sister's godchild, Bernadette Soubirous," the other nodded.

"The girl ought to be in school. I've never seen her there. How old are you, child?"

"I am fourteen next week, Monsieur," Bernadette informed him.

"You don't look above ten," the other disapproved.

"She suffers from constant bouts of asthma," the priest said. "And her environment has not been conducive to healthy development. Slum dwellers, you know. As I was telling you before my sister employs her as shepherdess to give the child a little country air and a few square meals."

"Madame Lagues is generous," the schoolmaster commented, "I trust you're grateful, Bernadette."

"Oh, yes, sir." She spoke cheerfully, for she loved Madame Lagues even if she did frequently lose her temper.

"The child has cause to be grateful," Monsieur Aravant said. "My sister was telling me that the father, from owning a mill of his own, has sunk to an occasional day's work as a labourer. The mother does what she can, but it's a case of too many children and a drop too much to drink on occasion."

"Wine is the curse of the poor," the schoolmaster said.

"It's cheaper than bread," the priest said wryly. "Who's to blame an overworked, hungry woman for snatching dreams out of a bottle? Louise Casterot was a good-looking girl when she wed François Soubirous. Now she's not much past thirty and looks ten years older."

"Then she must have been doubly glad to get one of the children off her hands. I hope you're a good girl and help your kind godmother."

"She's a very obedient child," Monsieur Aravant said.

"But a little schooling wouldn't go amiss. Can you read and write?" enquired Monsieur Barbet.

"No, sir."

"My sister gives her a lesson in the evenings, but the results are not encouraging."

"I hope you're not lazy!" Monsieur Barbet exclaimed.

"No sir, but I'm very stupid," Bernadette informed him.

"Are you indeed?" The schoolmaster raised amused eyebrows. "Do you speak French?"

"A few words, sir, but we talk Bigourdan."

"As do most of the local peasants," Monsieur Barbet gave an exasperated shrug. "How can one introduce them to the glories of Racine, of Moliere, when they chatter in their barbarous patois all the time?"

"You should try getting them to follow the Latin of the Mass," Monsieur Aravant said wryly. "This girl ought to have made her first Holy Communion a year ago, but no attempt seems to have been made to prepare her for it. I'm doing what I can, but my other duties take me far afield, as you know, and she needs individual coaching. Mind, she always comes to church."

"Don't you want to make your First Holy Communion?" the schoolmaster enquired.

"Yes, sir, but I can't say the Catechism yet," Bernadette explained.

"Why on earth not?"

"I can't remember the words," she said tranquilly. "I can say the holy rosary, but I get muddled up with everything else."

"She tries very hard," Monsieur Aravant excused her,

"but the intelligence is lacking, I fear."

"But you take good care of the sheep?"

"I watch they don't stray," she said, "but Pigou rounds them up and drives them back to the lower meadow at the end of the day."

"What else can you do? Sew? Cook? Take charge of babies?"

"I look after my brothers and my sister," she said doubtfully.

"How many are there?"

"Six of us, sir, but two of my brothers died when they were little. I'm the eldest, sir."

"And the stupid one."

"Yes, sir. They call me dumbell."

"You don't appear to mind."

"Not when it's true," the child said placidly.

The schoolmaster frowned, peering at the round face framed in the white capulet hood of the woollen cape. There was something about the girl that pleased him despite himself. Her voice was deeper and richer than might have been expected from someone so young and small.

"You'd best be getting the sheep down," Monsieur Aravant reminded her.

"Yes, Monsieur le Curé. Monsieur." Again came the neat little curtsey and the girl was scrambling up the track towards the barn.

"We'd best be getting back ourselves," Monsieur Barbet said. "I've had enough exercise for one day."

"And the child?" The priest spoke eagerly as they turned and began a leisurely descent.

"So that's why we came this way! You wanted a report on your protégée!"

"Hardly that," Monsieur Aravant disclaimed. "My sister took her in as a favour to the Soubirous. Marie looked after her before when she was a baby and Louise Soubirous was expecting another. I have little to do with the girl."

"But you wanted me to meet her. Why?"

"I wondered if you noticed anything unusual about her."

"She has a strong voice for her size," the other said.

"It is her eyes," the priest said slowly. "There is something about her eyes that haunts me whenever I meet her, or see her in church. I can't explain it or understand it, but that child doesn't look *at* you. She looks *through* you as if she were searching for something. My sister says she's affectionate, obedient, and so dull that it's useless trying to teach her anything, but I don't. I don't know."

"What exactly are you trying to say?" Monsieur Barbet asked with heavy patience.

"I saw Melanie Calvat once," the other said abruptly.

"The visionary of La Sallette!"

"An ignorant peasant like the Soubirous child, and with the same expression in her eyes."

"Visionaries are apt to cause trouble," Monsieur Barbet said dryly. "Didn't Melanie enter Carmel and cause an uproar there by biting the Novice Mistress? And don't forget Rose Tamisier with her fake bleeding statue and contrived stigmata. The Archbishop won't thank you for digging up another miracle worker."

"You're probably right." The priest clapped his companion on the shoulder and hastened his step.

With the sheep housed and Pigou enjoying a large bowl of scraps, Bernadette clattered across the yard in her wooden sabots and entered the farmhouse. The Lagues were already at supper but her own was between two plates by the fire. She took her place at the long table and ate slowly, Madame Lagues gave her maize bread and a lump of cheese to eat up in the fields at midday, but the evening meal was more substantial. Tonight there was roast pork and an apple tart.

It smelled delicious, but she ate cautiously, knowing that within an hour she would probably vomit it up again. It was uncomfortable having a weak digestion, but she was accustomed to it and never bothered to grumble.

"Fetch the book, child." Madame Lagues had taken her seat by the fire. She spoke in a tone of resignation, the reading lessons being as difficult for her as for her pupil. But her brother had hinted recently that she was neglecting her duty to her godchild, and Bernadette was eager to learn.

Eager, but useless! Marie Lagues tapped her foot impatiently as the girl stared at the printed page, her tongue between her teeth, her narrow forefinger stabbing at the first letter.

"Well, what is it then? I told you yesterday! It's not possible to forget so quickly."

Something was tugging at Bernadette's attention. The letters before her eyes blurred and ran together like the river Gave that twisted around her home town of Lourdes. She was needed in Lourdes because there was something there to be done that only she could do. The prompting had come before but recently it had become almost impossible to resist. She had to grip the edge of her stool to prevent herself from running down the road towards the town three kilometres away.

"Bernadette! Have you lost your wits or are you being deliberately obstinate?"

"I'm sorry." The dark eyes blinked. "What did you want?"

"I want you to read me one letter from that page."

"Yes. Which one?"

"The first one, unless you've taken to reading books backward."

"I can't read any of them," Bernadette said. "I can see they are different shapes, but I can't fit sounds to them."

"The girl can see they're different shapes!" Marie Lagues appealed to the rest of the family. "Two months' instruction and she's learned that much!"

"She's tired," Monsieur Lagues advised, puffing at his pipe. "Let her alone, Marie."

"Are you tired or just stupid?" Madame Lagues demanded.

"Just stupid, Madame."

"And insolent!" The book was snatched from her and flung to the floor. "Don't you have good food here, and a warm bed, and plenty of time to be out in the fresh air? Do you imagine I enjoy trying to drum a little knowledge into your head?"

"No, Madame."

"And yet you do nothing right. You cannot follow the simplest order unless it is repeated twice! Are you listening to me?"

The tugging was so strong it was like a pain. At the back of her eyes something flickered into life and was gone.

"Can you do anything without having to be pushed into it?" Madame Lagues was despairing.

Bernadette gazed at her, wanting to please.

"I can love," she said at last. "It's all I can do, Madame, for I am truly very stupid."

ONE

"She begged so hard to be allowed to stay at home that I didn't have the heart to refuse her," Louise was saying.

She had gone over to a neighbour's house for a brief gossip to enliven the morning, and was rocking the baby while her friend boiled some milk for him. Justin Buohohorts was a delicate child, subject to alarming convulsions, and the local women often held agitated discussions on the best way of dealing with them. Louise herself was glad to sit down. She'd been on her feet since dawn, scrubbing down the walls of Le Cachot with a new preparation that was reputed to kill fleas. Half of her time, she reflected drearily, was spent in trying to keep her family and the room where they lived decently clean. She seemed to be perpetually boiling water and dragging a toothcomb through the children's hair.

Yet at seventeen, when she had married François Soubirous, she had been the prettiest of the four Casterot girls, with soft blue eyes and fair hair that curled about her temples. Life had been happy at the Boly Mill with a steady stream of customers and plenty of gay, social evenings. Sometimes she wondered when it had all begun to go wrong. Perhaps it had been when her mother, who had managed the housekeeping, decided to move out, or perhaps it had begun when her sister, Bernarde, had come home weeping and pregnant. Perhaps it had all begun when a candle had caught fire and dripped hot wax down the front of Louise's bodice, making it painful for her to feed the baby, especially as she was already expecting again. That second baby had died and although Louise loved Bernadette and was glad to have her home from her foster-mother at Bartres, there was always an empty space in her heart when she thought of her little, dead son. Her next child had been another girl and then had come another boy. She had thought of him as replacing his dead brother and had given him the same name of Jean, but he had barely lived two years and died when she was heavy with the weight of another child. She had named him Jean too, and so far, unlike his two little namesakes, he had proved sturdy and resilient.

But with Maman involved in the affairs of the rest of the family, for another sister had borne a child out of wedlock, there had been nobody to advise her how to budget, or how to chase up the debts that so many customers owed. And François had left matters in her hands and gone off fishing, leaving the machinery to rust. She would never forget that terrible day when he had come screaming into the kitchen with a piece of rusty metal embedded so deeply in his eye that he never after regained the sight of it. What with doctor's bills for that, and more money to be spent on patent cures for Bernadette's asthma, and a couple of wretched harvests it was no wonder, Louise thought, that they had fallen behind with the rent and had been forced to move to a much smaller mill. Justin had been born here, and Louise hoped secretly that he would remain the youngest, for her pregnancies were hard and every extra mouth a disaster, but François was a vigorous man with normal appetites and it was a great sin to limit one's family.

In the year of Justin's birth cholera had swept through the town, and Bernadette had almost died of it. By the time the family came out of quarantine half the customers had drifted elsewhere and, with the rent again outstanding, they had moved to an even smaller mill.

That winter of eighteen-fifty-six had been a harsh and

bitter season. Maman had died, and Louise's share of the money she left only served to pay off the more pressing debts. It had been a relief when Bernarde, married now and with a flourishing little tavern, had taken Bernadette back with her for a few months. The new venture had been a failure too, and the Soubirous had left the tiny mill and found lodgings in the town. That had been a lean year with drought sending corn prices rocketing, and work so scarce that they often went to bed hungry and finally endured the humiliation of eviction.

"I remember when we came here," Louise said, rocking the baby gently and talking more to herself than to her friend. "It was spring and the blossom was thick as snow. We piled what we had on a cart and Monsieur Maisongrosse lent us a horse to pull it. And we arrived and went into the cachot and all the blossom was gone."

As long as she lived she would never forget her first sight of that dark room with water running down the walls, and black beetles scurrying over the floor, and one small barred window that looked out over a tiny yard piled with dung. It had been the town gaol once until the authorities declared it insanitary, but at least they lived there rent free.

"Is François working today?" the other asked.

Louise shook her head. "He is not well," she excused. "He had hoped for a carting job, but there is nothing available."

"So he's in bed." Croisine Buohohorts spoke without expression, but Louise flushed miserably.

"He works very hard," she said defensively, "but so few will employ him since our little trouble."

The little trouble had consisted of nine days locked up in the new gaol while the police tried to discover if François Soubirous was guilty or not guilty of stealing some flour and a plank of wood. In the end they had let him go for lack of evidence, but François was still bitter about the affair. He had never stolen so much as a cup of flour, and the plank had been lying in the gutter for anybody to pick up. Officially, however, he was a man with a record, and when casual work was unobtainable he lay in bed with the blankets pulled over his head.

"We all have our troubles," Croisine said. "My little baby won't live many months. Dr Douzous as good as told me so on his last visit."

"What do doctors know about illness?" Louise scoffed. "Why, your Justin is improving. I see it."

"Do you think so, truly?"

"He has a spot of colour in his cheeks," Louise said stoutly. "Mark my words, but he'll improve as the year goes on."

"He's my last one," her friend said wistfully. "I couldn't endure losing another. Sometimes it seems that everything I love dies on me."

"Come, that's foolish talk!"

Louise rose and laid the child in the cradle. "Why, you've only the one to worry over! Look at me with four of them. I tell you Jean and Justin are like a couple of monkeys. No knowing what they'll get up to the second my back is turned. And Toinette is no better sometimes. She and that Baloume are always into some mischief or other."

"She'll turn out bad that girl," Croisine predicted gloomily. "Ah, but you ought to have made Bernadette stay at Bartres."

"She was so anxious to come back to Lourdes," Louise said. "And she's a good help to me. The boys generally behave themselves when she minds them. I wish she could get over her cough though. She kept us awake most of the night with her choking, and she can't eat the maize bread at all. I was hoping to buy some white bread for her, but there's no cleaners wanted at the market-place today. I went down earlier to see."

"Have a drop of something before you go," Croisine urged, watching her friend begin to pull on her patched cape.

"I ought not," Louise said, but she eyed the squat jug wistfully.

"A swallow to keep out the cold."

"Just a sip then."

The wine was sour and rough on her tongue, but its red glow warmed her stomach. She drained the short measure, virtuously shook her head when Croisine pushed across the jug again, and went out into the street.

It was a damp, grey morning without a breath of wind. The steep, narrow streets of the ancient town wound down to the river that crashed against the ramparts of the castle and then dashed headlong to the flat meadows that lay beyond the cobbles and the slate roofs. There were seasons when Lourdes was beautiful, its fields starred with primroses and tiny wild lilies, the mountain sparkling with snow so white that it merged into the hyacinth of the sky. February was not such a season, for it had rained steadily for days. The houses with their shuttered windows and peeling doors looked small and mean and bits of rubbish floated in the deep gutters.

A young man in clerical garb was walking down the street, Louise recognised one of the local curates and dropped a polite curtsey. L'Abbé Pomian was a good natured young man who gave light penances after Confession. She would have liked to speak to him, but he passed with only a brief inclination of the head. She would have liked to enquire how Toinette was getting on at school. She had been attending the school run by the Sisters of Charity for several months now, and had picked up a little French. She had a good memory and could already spell out her name and recite some poems she'd learned. She might do well for herself if she got a little education. If François or I had ever learned to read and write, Louise thought, we could have kept the accounts straight and not lost the mill. Her mother had been able to read and count a little and she had tried to teach her daughters, but Louise had been too pretty and too lively to sit still for very long.

Pretty! Her lips curled a little as she looked down at her chapped and calloused hands, the wedding ring cutting deeply into the swollen knuckle of her finger. Market-day was usually a busy day for there were stalls to be cleaned if one got down early enough, and at the end of the day there would often be damaged vegetables being sold off cheaply. They had eaten a bowl of onion soup early that morning, and she had saved a piece of white bread from a loaf she'd bought the day before, but there was no other food in the cachot, and no prospect of earning any that day.

She gave a resigned, dispirited shrug and turned into Las Petits Fosses, thinking as she always did that Street of Little Stones was an exact description of the life she led.

A short dark passage led from the street into the room where the Soubirous lived. It was dim here even on a bright day and this morning the small grate was empty, the wood having been used up. Over the narrow mantelshelf hung the big wooden crucifix with the rosary draped across it. A tall cupboard at one side of the fireplace held the dishes she had salvaged from her old home; at the other side was a small stone sink. The only other items of furniture in the room were two thick mattresses and a tin chest containing a few items of clothing.

François was lying on one of the mattresses, his head half-buried in the blanket. He had given his share of soup to three-year-old Justin who had cried for more. He was a fretful, wailing child who hung onto her skirts and was forever wanting to be carried. The soup had evidently satisfied him, for he was curled up against his father's back with his eyes closed and his thumb in his mouth.

Toinette and Jean were in the back skipping with a long piece of rope. Bernadette sat by the window, watching them, or at least with her head turned in that direction for the face she presented to Louise was as blankly indifferent as ever.

She had in fact been thinking about school, and wishing she had not been kept at home that day. She had missed so many years that even though she had been put in the lowest form of the lowest class she would never catch up. As the lessons were given in French she had to strain her ears to catch a familiar word, and guess at the meaning of all the words in between, and on the rare occasions when she was invited to answer a question she never seemed to give the answer that was wanted.

Only the previous day she had landed herself in trouble. It had been raining hard but a pale sun had struggled through the clouds by mid-afternoon, and the rain drops against the pane sparkled like crystals. It was so beautiful that she was caught up in the sheer joy of watching those jewels of water and light.

"Soubirous!" The teacher's voice jerked her back.

"Yes, Sister." She sat up, her eyes fixed obediently upon the spare black and white figure of the nun.

"I asked you a question. Is it possible for you to give me the honour of your attention for a few minutes?"

"Yes, Sister."

"I asked you to tell me what you know about the Holy Trinity."

Bernadette stared at her blankly.

"You have heard of the Holy Trinity, I take it?"

"I think so," Bernadette said doubtfully.

"Then perhaps you will tell me what *It* is." The nun rattled the beads at her girdle and tapped her foot.

"It is—God, I think."

"And what is God?" Sister asked. "Come now, you attend the holy sacrifice of the Mass every Sunday, don't you? Tell me then what is God?"

"God is——" Completely at a loss Bernadette chewed her lip miserably.

"God is what?"

"Loving," Bernadette said. "God is Loving."

"God is a threefold Spirit, co-equal and co-existent, without beginning or end," the nun said briskly. "Do you understand that, girls?"

Every hand in the class except Bernadette's was raised. She gazed at the others wistfully, wondering if she would ever reach their standard.

"Soubirous, don't you understand the Holy Trinity yet?" Sister was demanding.

"No, Sister."

The nun looked briefly and eloquently up to the ceiling and set her mouth firmly. When she spoke her voice was icily sweet.

"Then, Soubirous, I suggest you stay here in class and meditate on the Holy Trinity while the others go out to play. The rain has eased and a little exercise will do you good. What is it now, child?"

"I don't know how to meditate," Bernadette said.

"Empty your mind of everything but the Holy Trinity. After break I'll ask you what thoughts arose."

The others filed obediently out. Bernadette leaned her elbows on the desk and tried to think of nothing but the Holy Trinity. That must be the Father, the Son, and the Holy Ghost, she decided. God the Father had made the world; God the Son had lived in it, and she was not at all sure what God the Holy Ghost did, except that it must have been something very important.

The sun was shining more brightly now, and the raindrops were vanishing like stars just before dawn. There was a warmth on the back of her head and her shoulders, and the soreness in her chest was easing. The voices of the other girls in the yard at the side of the school were muted. It was peaceful here, as peaceful as it had been at Bartres high in the meadow.

"And what have you found out about the Holy Trinity?" Sister was demanding.

The peace was shattered as the others trooped back.

"Nothing, Sister."

"Soubirous, you've sat there for fifteen minutes! You must have been thinking about something!"

"Sheep," Bernadette said reluctantly.

"Sheep! What have sheep to do with the Holy Trinity?"

"Nothing, Sister."

"But you were thinking about them. What else entered your thoughts?"

"Stars," Bernadette said, catching at the memory of a fleeting image.

"So, after fifteen minutes of concentrated meditation, you come up with sheep and stars!" The beads rattled furiously in the nun's narrow hand. "Come, you must have something better to offer than that."

"No, Sister."

"Sometimes," the nun said tensely, "I am tempted to wonder why the Good Lord saw fit to afflict me with such a burden as you. Indeed, I am even tempted to wonder why He ever made you at all."

"I suppose," said Bernadette helpfully, "because He'd nothing better to do at the time."

She had been sent to stand in the corridor after that which meant she'd missed the rest of the lesson anyway. It was a pity because she wanted so very badly to learn, but at least her absence made the day easier for poor Sister.

And today, with Papa in one of his dark, abstracted moods and Maman looking for work, she hadn't been able to attend school at all. It was close in the room and the walls still smelled of the stuff with which Maman had washed the walls down.

"I shall have to fetch wood," Louise said. "There may be some in the Savy meadow, and we can perhaps earn a few sous later if we sell the wood."

"I'll get the wood," Toinette sang from the doorway.

At twelve she was already taller than Bernadette, with curly brown hair and eyes that slanted attractively at the corners.

"Not all by yourself. Take one of the other girls with you."

"I'll go for wood." Jeanne Abadie, who was nicknamed Baloume, appeared behind Toinette, one of her little brothers slung from her hip.

"Well, I'm not sure." Louise hesitated, disapproving of the hoydenish Baloume but not wishing to be unkind.

"Do let us go," Toinette said eagerly. "We might find some bones, too. They fetch more than wood."

"Very well, then. Baloume, take your brother to your maman and tell her where you're going. Take the big basket, Toinette. And where are you off to, Missy?"

"To put on my sabots and go for wood," Bernadette said.

"And have you coughing again all night? You'll stay right here, out of the cold!"

"I won't cough," Bernadette said earnestly. "At Bartres I went out every day with the sheep. Please, maman!"

"Put your stockings on then and your capulet," Louise

ordered.

She didn't usually give in so easily, but François was stirring and she had no food to offer him if he woke.

It was good to be in the fresh air even though the clouds hung low. Baloume and Toinette were already skipping ahead, their baskets swinging. Bernadette followed more slowly, lifting her face to the sky. There were no gleams of sunshine today, but the strange tugging had begun again deep inside her.

They were crossing the bridge now that led to the forest trail. On the banks of the river an old woman was rinsing tripe. The girls knew her as Tata, who lived by begging, sleeping where she could find a space. Sometimes she sang and muttered to herself, the ragged headdress she wore bobbing up and down. Baloume and Toinette squeezed past, being secretly a little afraid of her craziness. Bernadette paused to curtsey. She knew, without knowing how she knew, that Tata had once known a different kind of life, and that sunk so low that even the Soubirous pitied her, she was nonetheless a lady.

"Where are you off to then?" Tata enquired, squatting back on her heels.

"To get wood," Baloume said over her shoulder.

"Try La Fitte's meadow."

"It's private," Bernadette said. "People might say we were stealing."

Never would she forget those terrible days when her father had been locked up in gaol.

"Try the canal turn then, over at Massabielle."

The girls hesitated. The great rock of Massabielle rose above the Savy meadow separated from it by the river which met the mill canal at the tip of the meadow. It was a desolate place, the rock hollowed out at one side into a deep cave, its floor silted up with sand and acorns. Pigs were brought there sometimes to graze, but most people avoided the place without knowing why. There was a local legend that once there had been killings there, strange, dark rites long forgotten. But nobody knew the exact story nor even if it were true. There were many tales told in the district about witches and fairies and dark powers locked deep in the earth.

"Shall we go to Massabielle then?" Toinette asked Bernadette.

The elder girl stood still. The tugging inside her had gone as if it had never been. She was not even sure why she had been so anxious to come out.

"Let's go," Baloume said impatiently. "She can catch up if she likes."

Bernadette curtsied again to old Tata. She wished she had something to give the old woman, but her pockets were empty. The others had run on across the lower footbridge that by-passed the Savy mill. She followed them more cautiously, her wooden sabots slipping on the damp wood.

The meadow was wet and muddy. Her feet squelched as she plodded across it towards the wide, rushing stream. The water was low enough to wade through but it looked cold. The others were already splashing across, sabots and baskets above their heads, squealing.

"I can't get my feet wet," she called, "or Maman will be angry. Can you make a chair of your arms to carry me?"

"Go back in that freezing water? Not likely!" At the other side Toinette and Baloume were replacing their sabots.

"Can you put stepping stones?"

"Stay there!" Toinette shouted. "We'll not be long!"

"Don't leave me alone here! Baloume! Baloume, wait!"

"Oh—piss off!" Baloume yelled.

"Don't swear!"

"Pisspot!" the other retorted. "Stay there, goody-goody."

But she wanted to be with them. She didn't want to be

left alone with only the rushing water and the dark cave and the grey sky. For an instant it was as if Massabielle threatened her whole life.

TWO

Toinette and Baloume were moving away among the trees, bending to fill their baskets, their chatter growing fainter. Bernadette sat down on a large rock and stared after them miserably. It was always the same. She was slower and more stupid than anybody she knew. She had never resented the fact and she did not resent it now, but she was wrapped in a great loneliness of spirit.

There were no bits of driftwood on this side of the stream, but the piles of broken branches and gleaming bones on the far side tempted her. If she ran very quickly through the cold water she might escape catching a chill.

She took off her wooden sabots and began to unroll the thick white stockings Louise insisted upon her wearing. In her ears there sounded abruptly a rushing of wind, but when she looked up, anticipating the patter of rain, the landscape was still and grey, not a blade of grass stirring. The first stocking off she bent to the other and heard again the strange rushing noise. The pine-trees were so motionless that they looked as if somebody had painted them against the sky, but the bushes and creepers that overhung the cave were tossing wildly. The cave itself was dim, but in a narrower cleft at the side, about twelve feet from the ground, a light was shining. It was like a great crystal and at the heart of the crystal something or someone was waiting.

Scrambling to her feet she rubbed her eyes disbelievingly, but when she risked another glance the light was still there, dimmed to a golden glow, and in its centre stood a very young lady. Bernadette could see her quite clearly, and it was evident that the lady could see her too for she bowed and smiled.

She was a very tiny lady, the child decided, and her dress and face were as white as a candle. The only touches of colour about her were her blue girdle and two yellow roses on her feet. Bare feet, Bernadette realized. Ordinary feet didn't have roses growing out of them, nor were ordinary eyes so intensely blue that the colour of them blazed across the intervening distance.

When one was nervous and confused it was advisable, L'Abbé Pomian had told the Catechism class, to kneel down and recite the rosary. Her eyes fixed cautiously on the being in the cleft of rock, she knelt and took out of her pocket the string of black beads that Louise had bought for her down in the market one day.

The gesture was evidently pleasing to the lady for she smiled more brilliantly and held up a long rosary of her own, its pearls linked by gold with a gold cross pendant on it.

Bernadette moved her hand in preparation for the sign of the cross that marked the beginning of the devotion, but her fingers were stiff and heavy, so heavy that her arm dropped again to her side. The lady was raising her own arm, crossing herself in a slow and stately fashion. The great cross formed by the slender hand hung glittering on the air.

Bernadette could move her own arm again without difficulty. She crossed herself slowly and began the prayers, the beads slipping through her fingers, each bead a ray of light that reached out to the greater light surrounding the lady.

Baloume, glancing back across the stream, exclaimed in disbelief. "Hey! your sister's saying her prayers!"

"I never saw her do that before," Toinette said, puzzled.

"She's getting up from her knees." Baloume set down her basket and stared. "She's taken off her stockings and she's coming across the stream!"

"She'll catch her death," Toinette said gloomily, in imitation of Louise.

"The water isn't cold!" Bernadette exclaimed. "It's warm as dish-water! And there's so much wood here. Maman will be pleased."

She was darting about flinging sticks and bones into her basket.

"You'd better slow down or you'll be ill," Toinette warned.

"Let's climb up above the rock and go home through the woods," Bernadette said, and without waiting for an answer ran lightly up the stony track.

The others scrambled after her, panting, for the way was steep, but when they hauled their baskets onto the high path Bernadette was striding ahead of them, the laden basket swinging from her hand. She turned as Baloume shouted and waited for them, her face only slightly flushed.

"You're not coughing!" Toinette accused.

"How did you get up the path so quickly?" Baloume wanted to know.

"I just walked," Bernadette said calmly.

Inside she was tingling with excitement. The lady in the crystal of light had vanished as suddenly as she had appeared when the prayers were finished, but the glory of her coming had remained with the girl.

"Did something happen down there at Massabielle?" Baloume asked with a flash of shrewdness.

"It might have done." Her lips curved into an impish smile.

"They say the place is haunted," Toinette said. "What did you see?"

"You won't tell. Promise not to tell. Cross your heart and cut your throat and promise!"

"We won't tell. What did you see?"

Bernadette hesitated, looking from one to the other. Part of her wanted to keep the little lady to herself; part of her wanted to share what she had seen with the other girls.

"I saw a little young lady," she said at last, "in a white dress with a blue girdle and yellow roses on her feet."

"You little liar!" Snatching a branch from her basket, Toinette hit out at her sister.

"I did see her. Cross my heart!"

"You're making it up to be important," Baloume said in disgust.

"Then I'm not saying any more. And you promised not to tell!"

Bernadette stuck her chin in the air and marched ahead again.

At the cachot she dumped her wood and accepted the piece of white bread Louise had saved for her. Toinette, coming in after her, was promptly hauled into the corner to have her hair combed. She stood, restless under her mother's hands, watching from under her lashes as Bernadette wandered out into the passage again.

"What are you fidgeting about?" Louise enquired.

"Don't say that I said, but Bernadette saw something white over at Massabielle," Toinette whispered.

"You're making it up."

"No, maman. She said she saw a lady who vanished."

"Stuff and nonsense! Bernadette!" Louise raised her voice.

"Yes, maman." Bernadette came obediently, still chewing.

"What's all this about a lady at Massabielle?"

"There was a lady," Bernadette said, darting a reproachful glance at her sister.

"A visitor?"

"I don't think so, maman. She was in the little cave at the side of the big one, and there was light all around her."

Louise grabbed a broom leaning in the corner and brought it down hard, first across Bernadette's back, then across the younger girl's shoulders.

"One for telling lies, and one for telling tales!" she said crossly. "Now get down to the market and sell the wood."

The clatter of sabots retreated into the street again. From the bed François said, "The child doesn't tell lies. She's too stupid."

"Then she imagined it," Louise said wearily. "She's at the age for imagining."

She had, she considered, enough troubles without ladies in white complicating her life.

"A pretend game," she said. "It'll be a new craze tomorrow."

Some of the wood had spilled out of the baskets. She gathered them up and piled them in the fireplace. The sale of the wood would provide a loaf and she intended to light a comfortable fire.

Later, as they recited the rosary together, Louise glanced at her elder daughter and saw with dismay that tears were pouring silently down the round face.

"Are you sick, Bernadette?" she asked sharply.

"No, maman."

"Then what are you crying about?"

"The lady was beautiful," Bernadette sobbed. "I have to see her again, maman."

"You have to do nothing of the kind," Louise said firmly. "It was a dream you had, that's all. Just a dream. You have to put it right out of your mind. Now let's get to bed. We've a long day tomorrow, and a chance your father might find some work."

The next day would be school again. Perhaps maman was right and it had only been a dream. But surely dreams were not so vivid and didn't stay in the mind so long. There was an aching deep inside her, as if she had lost a friend, but that was stupid because the little lady had never even spoken.

Others evidently had spoken, for Bernadette, arriving at school the next morning, was conscious at once of the groups of whispering girls in the playground. Baloume hadn't kept her promise either. It was a shame because now the lady no longer belonged to herself alone. But that was selfish. Many of the children were as poor as she was, and had as much right as anyone to see something beautiful.

"Tell us about the lady!" A small girl was tugging at her sleeve.

"Was it a fairy? Did you see a fairy?" somebody asked eagerly.

"Baloume says you ran up the steep path without coughing!"

For once she was the centre of flattering, not contemptuous, attention. Some of the bigger girls grew bored and wandered away, but the little ones listened, their mouths and eyes opened. Yet she was glad when the bell put an end to the gossiping, and she could take her place in class.

Not that the dream or whatever it was had made any difference to her stupidity! She sat, with hanging head, while Sister raised her eyes to Heaven, rattled her beads, and cried despairingly that her life was certain to be shortened by a certain idiot Soubirous.

Perhaps it was better to put what had happened out of her mind. But the memory of it was so clear and her yearning to return to Massabielle so strong that she could fix her attention on nothing.

It was useless to try to explain anything to her parents, for she could understand nothing of it herself. The lady had been real for she had smiled and bowed and moved her hands. But she had appeared and vanished in a flash, her feet had been bare with the roses apparently growing out of the flesh, so she couldn't possibly be real. All she knew was that she wanted to go back to Massabielle.

The next day L'Abbé Pomian, shifting cramped legs in the confessional, bent his head to the dark grating and prepared to listen to another stumbling recital of faults. He was tired and hungry and thought a little wistfully about supper.

"Bless me, Father, for I have sinned."

A girl's voice, whispering huskily in patois. He leaned closer.

"I saw something white like a lady."

"Something evil, my child?"

"I don't think so, but it troubles me."

"Tell me about it," the curate murmured, and forgot his supper as he listened.

It was not until after the meal, however, that he had the opportunity of seeking out the priest who was taking his usual stroll along the Argeles road, and they talked at first of other matters. L'Abbé Peyramale had little patience with the trivial and fanciful. He heard his curate's tale in silence, with no more than an occasional sharp glance from under his beetling brows.

"She gave me leave to consult you," L'Abbé Pomian finished. "Her name is Bernadette Soubirous."

"Never heard of her," L'Abbé Peyramale said briefly.

"A slum child, but she told the story so simply. 'She came with a gust of wind.' That was how she put it. A lady in a white dress. You don't think——?"

"I don't think anything," his superior interrupted.

"But as clergymen, don't you feel we ought to do something?"

"We'll wait and see," L'Abbé Peyramale said. "Now I return to this meeting of the Children of Mary. . . ."

After Mass on Sunday a few people lingered to gossip.

Sunday was a working day when the observance of the Sabbath had been performed, but a few women nodded their shawled heads together.

"A bit feeble-minded if you ask me, but a good little sort."

"My Catherine wants to go over herself to find this lady."

"Baloume says there was nothing there, but the Soubirous girl had a funny look on her face."

"Watch out! Here comes François Soubirous."

"He's cleaning out the livery stables for Monsieur Cazenave today."

"That'll put a little food inside them. Hand to mouth, those children live."

"And Louise was such a pretty girl."

Francois, polishing harness, looked up as a group of children clattered in.

"What happened? Is it an earthquake?" he demanded.

"Can Bernadette go with us to Massabielle to find the white lady?"

"Ask my wife," he said shortly.

"We did, and she said to ask you," Toinette shrilled.

François straightened up and frowned across at his elder daughter who stood on the fringe of the group. She looked nervous and uncertain as if she almost wished he would forbid the expedition.

"Do you want to go?" he asked.

"I told the little ones they could see her," she told him.

"And we've got holy water to throw at her in case she's the devil in disguise," another girl said eagerly.

"Let them go," Cazenave advised. "A bit of a lark won't hurt them."

"Very well, then. Straight there and straight back," François decided.

Bernadette drew a deep breath for all the world as if she were steeling herself to something, and then turned and dashed out of the stable ahead of the others. For two days she had wondered if the lady were real or a dream. Now she would find out, for dreams surely wouldn't come when she was determined to stay awake and the other children were there.

She outpaced them, taking the forest path and running down the steep slope to the cave. Today the stream and the flat Savy meadows were at her back, and she knelt on the sand and grass only a few yards from the cave.

"There's nobody there," someone said in disappointment.

"We'll say a rosary," she decided.

Some of the little ones knelt with her. Baloume and a few of her cronies remained on top of the cliff, peering down at the empty niche.

It had been a dream after all. The lady wasn't here. Bernadette tried to fix her mind upon the prayers, but her eyes could not help scanning the cleft in the rock. If she could only call back a little of the dream to please the others.

The crystal filled the black space, then dimmed to a golden glow as the small, white-gowned figure became sharp and clear.

"She's here. Look, she's up there!" she exclaimed.

The others were staring blankly from the cave to her and back again.

"You'd better throw some holy water at her," one of the children said.

It seemed impolite, but she threw the contents of the little bottle towards the rock, saying in a high, nervous voice.

"If from God, stay. If from the devil, go away."

"I can't see anything at all," one girl piped up.

"But she's there. Oh, you must be able to see her!" Bernadette pulled the child closer.

"I'll do in your lady!" Baloume called from the top of the cliff, and flung down a stone. It crashed against the niche and rolled past to the ground.

For an instant the white figure vanished, and then the crystal grew so large and so dazzling that it blotted out the world.

"Bernadette! Did the stone hit you? Why don't you answer?"

"She's dead," Catherine said uncertainly.

"She's still on her knees. Dead folk lie down!"

"She's smiling. What is she smiling about?"

"Do get up! I can't move her!"

They clustered round, pulling and shoving, but the little figure with open eyes and folded hands was heavy as lead.

"Make her stop smiling!" one of the younger children said. "I don't like her smiling."

"The devil's taken her soul," another whispered.

"He's left only the empty shell!"

In a flurry of panic the children scattered, some clawing their way up the side of the cliff, others splashing through the water to the meadow beyond.

Antoine Nicolau straightened up from the log he was sawing and watched the children streaming across the fields towards him. It was evident from their shouts of consternation that some kind of accident had occurred. He threw down his saw and began to run, calling to his mother as he went, to follow him.

Outside the cave there was pandemonium, as the children milled about shouting hysterically. Two women had scrambled down from the path above and were trying, without success, to pull one of the girls to her feet. At a little distance Baloume stood with a white, scared look on her face.

"It's the Soubirous girl. She won't move," one of the women panted.

"A little thing like that!" Antoine splashed through the

stream and bent to peer at the girl. For a moment a cold shudder went through him, for the uplifted dark eyes and the fixed brilliant smile were unearthly.

"I threw a stone," Baloume said in a small voice, "but it didn't hit her."

"Then it's shocked her into a fit," one of the women said.

"It doesn't look like a fit," Antoine puzzled. "Her heart's beating steadily."

"She's no colour at all," Antoine's mother said, breathlessly joining them. "We'd better get her over to our place."

"I never saw anyone look like that before," Antoine said. "It doesn't look like a human child."

"Stop gaping at her, and let's get her to her feet," his mother said crossly.

It was no easy task. The child pulled against them constantly, her feet dragging. It was impossible to get her to close her eyes or to bend her head. And all the time she smiled the unearthly, brilliant smile.

It was a panting quartet of adults who finally dragged her across the threshold of the Nicolau house. They managed to lower her into a chair, but it was impossible to unclasp her hands. The fingers were locked in spasm, the palms tightly together.

"She is looking at something," Madame Nicolau said. "She is looking at it so hard that she sees nothing else."

But the look was fading. The dark eyes withdrew gradually from their abstraction, the hands unclasped, and a very ordinary little girl took one bewildered glance around the circle of faces and burst into noisy tears.

"What is it? What did you see?" Antoine demanded.

"A lady," Bernadette said. "I saw such a beautiful lady!"

"I'll give you a damn good hiding, let alone lady!" came a wrathful voice.

Louise, her apron awry, a shawl pulled over her head,

ran in with Toinette at her heels.

"Making a spectacle of yourself to amuse the neighbours! Do you enjoy disgracing us all? And your poor father only just back at work, too," Louise shouted.

"A moment ago, if only you'd seen her, she looked like an angel," Madame Nicolau interposed.

Overcome with temper and relief at discovering that no terrible accident had taken place. Louise sat down in an adjoining chair and began to weep.

"Troubles, and more troubles!" she fretted. "There's no end to it! They'll say the Soubirous have a crazy child now. Frightening everybody like that!"

"But I saw the lady, maman. I truly did see her again. She was clear as clear, and she's quite real."

"Not another word! Not one more word out of you about ladies in caves. And you won't go there again! Your little trips out to Massabielle are over."

"But I have to see her again, maman," Bernadette protested.

"I'm listening to no argument!" Louise said.

"You're coming home with me and you'll stay home, so you can save your breath. I'm not listening to you."

"But she wants me to come. She didn't say anything, but I know she does."

"Then she'll just have to wait. Out!" Louise had risen and was pulling her reluctant daughter to her feet. "Madame Nicolau, I can't apologise enough for all this fuss and bother."

"Don't be too hard on the child," the older woman pleaded. "She couldn't help what happened. I'm certain she saw something."

"Which is why she stays away from Massabielle in future," Louise said grimly. "You hear me, Bernadette?"

"Yes, maman." The spring had gone from her step and

her voice was listless. Slowly, her head bent, she trailed after her mother through the little group of chattering neighbours towards the bridge that led to the narrow streets of the town.

THREE

"Mamam, there are two ladies at the door," Jean said.

"Well, don't leave them standing there! Ask them to step in." Louise cast a harassed glance around the room and patted a stray wisp of hair into place.

"Madame Soubirous, forgive us for disturbing you at this hour." The squat little woman who pattered in wore a striped gown and a high bonnet festooned with cherries.

"Madame Millet." Louise, who went once or twice a week to clean at the local dressmaker's house, was flustered. At Madame Millet's side was her maid, Antoinette Peyret, clad more tastefully in dark blue.

"I'll come straight to the point," Madame Millet said briskly. "You were telling me yesterday how worried you were about your girl."

"She's quite herself again now," Louise said hastily, "and of course there'll be no more trips out to Massabielle."

"Mademoiselle Peyret and I have been talking it over," the dressmaker said. "It's clear your little girl saw something out at the cave, and we did wonder if it might not be my goddaughter, Elsa."

"Elsa Latapie?"

"She was buried in a white dress and veil," Madame Millet said, dabbing her eyes with a scrap of silk.

"I am so afraid that we may have neglected to do something, and her soul cannot rest. So, with your leave, we'll call for Bernadette early tomorrow, take her to Mass, and then walk over to Massabielle with her."

"I forbade her to go again," Louise began.

"As a special favour?" the dressmaker pleaded.

Louise twisted the corner of her apron. It would do her no good to deny the request. Madame Millet might be offended and employ another cleaner. On the other hand everything in her cried out against letting Bernadette return to the place where, according to all accounts, she had suffered some kind of fit.

From the corner François said, "If she's with the two ladies I see no harm in it."

"You hear that, Bernadette? You're to go with the ladies tomorrow morning."

"Yes, maman." The small figure drooping in the shadows spoke tonelessly.

Bernadette was not at all sure that she wanted to go to Massabielle after all. The three days since her second visit had been uncomfortable ones. Sister Damian had had some very cutting things to say about little show-offs who pretended to see angels and some of the older girls had bullied her at playtime. But if these ladies thought it was somebody called Elsa Latapie, then she might as well go with them to oblige.

The morning was cold and dark still when they came out of church. There were few people at a Thursday Mass unless it was a holiday of obligation, and the two crinolined ladies, the little shawled figure trotting between them, made their way unnoticed through the deserted streets.

"I've brought pen and ink and paper," Mademoiselle Peyret said, "so she can write down her name and instructions."

"And I have a holy candle," Madame Millet confided, "so we are very well prepared. Now you must let us know everything she says. Bernadette?"

She spoke to empty air for the child was speeding ahead of them towards the forest road. The ladies hurried after her, their wide skirts swaying.

"We'll never get down the cliff!" Madame Millet exclaimed when they arrived at the overhanging rocks.

"We'll slide," Mademoiselle Peyret said firmly, and suited action to words, uttering small squeals as she clutched at her billowing skirt.

"She's there," Bernadette said briefly, already on her knees.

The ladies peered up timidly at the dark cleft.

"We'll say the rosary," Madame decided, flopping on her own knees.

The prayers recited, Mademoiselle Peyret thrust the writing materials into Bernadette's hands. She was rather disappointed to see that the girl, far from being transfigured, looked stolid and faintly stupid.

She got up briskly enough however and went forward into the big cave itself, putting up her hand in an oddly commanding gesture. They could see her at the back of the cave standing on tiptoe with her hand up.

"Can we come in?" Madame called.

It was foolish but she felt for a moment as if she were intruding.

Bernadette's voice echoed queerly. "There's nothing to stop you, Madame."

"The paper's blank," Mademoiselle said, snatching it, and squinting up at a narrow ledge in the curving wall of rock. It was very dark but she could make out a narrow opening that twisted into a spiral passage which obviously led to the outer cleft.

"The lady laughed," Bernadette said: "She laughed and shook her head."

"Did she say anything?" Madame asked eagerly.

"She said, 'It's not necessary to write down what I have to say.' And then she said, 'Will you do me the grace of coming here every day for fifteen days?' "

"What language did she speak?" Mademoiselle asked.

"Bigourdan. She spoke to me as if I were a real grown up person," Bernadette said proudly.

"Is she still there?"

"Yes, Mademoiselle. She's smiling at you," Bernadette said promptly.

"Did she say anything else?"

"She said, 'I cannot promise to make you happy in this world, but I will in the next'," Bernadette reported.

"I don't see anything," Mademoiselle said bluntly.

"She's still there." Bernadette stared a moment longer at the high ledge, then said laconically, "She's gone now".

"It cannot have been Elsa," Madame Millet said.

"If you're telling lies God will punish you," Mademoiselle warned.

Dawn was flooding the cave. The two ladies stared around at the damp walls and stony floor, the bare creepers and coarse tufts of grass.

"You'd better come back and stay at my house," Madame decided. "Antoinette, will you go back to the cachot and tell Madame Soubirous that we're keeping the little girl with us for a while."

It was all very confusing, Bernadette thought. The previous Sunday she had been scolded for making a fool of herself, and now she was being invited to stay at a grand house. But the lady had come, and she had asked her to come back to Massabielle. That was what mattered. So as the two ladies questioned her eagerly she answered politely, her mind elsewhere.

Rather to her own surprise she slept badly in the wide, satin-hung bed. This was the first time she had ever slept in a room by herself, and though the carpets and plush curtains impressed her, she missed the warm bulk of Toinette next to her. The day had gone slowly, even though Madame Millet had given her a pile of books with pictures in them to look at. She had shown her pictures of Elsa Latapie, too, in a white dress and veil with a Missal in her hands, but Bernadette shook her head. That wasn't the lady.

"Is it possible that what you see is the Blessed Mother herself?" Madame Millet had ventured.

Bernadette had seen pictures of the Holy Mother and there was a statue in the parish church, but none of them resembled the being who came to Massabielle. When she referred to her Bernadette used the patois word, 'Aquero', which meant 'That thing'.

They were going to collect maman and Aunt Bernarde, and seven or eight other women clattered along with them. Aunt Bernarde had brought a holy candle with her too, and kept glaring at Madame Millet as if she suspected her of wanting to take all the credit. Louise was subdued and silent. Something beyond her comprehension was happening and she was being carried along in the tide of events like a bit of paper thrown into the Gave.

When they reached the cave she knelt awkwardly, glancing from the cleft in the rock to her child's face. A change was coming over it, so rapidly that it was as if the obedient, slightly stupid girl whom she had reared was turning before her eyes into someone quite different. All the colour had gone from the round face and the skin was drawn so tightly over the bones that the blue veins could clearly be seen. The dark eyes had lost their habitually dreamy expression and were fixed blazingly on the empty ledge. It was certain that she saw something or someone.

And then it was over. The eyes resumed their docile dreaming look, colour returned to the cheeks, and the strange ecstatic being was her own daughter again.

"Bernadette must go home with her mother," Aunt Bernarde was saying officiously. "You've been very kind, Madame Millet, but the child is our responsibility and her place is with her own family."

'Did the lady say anything to you?" Louise asked.

"No, maman."

"But you want to come back tomorrow, I suppose?"

"Yes, maman."

Louise threw up her hands. "If it has to be it has to be," she said. "But I can't see any good coming of any of it. There'll be scandal, mark my words, and Heaven knows who'll give your father a job then."

"Are you sure the lady said nothing?" Aunt Bernarde asked, taking her niece's arm, as if she feared she might run away straight back to the dressmaker's house.

"There were other voices," Bernadette said. "Voices from under the river."

"Under the river! What on earth do you mean?" her aunt exclaimed.

"Voices shouting and snarling under the water. Aquero looked towards them and frowned, and the voices went away."

"I heard nothing," Aunt Bernarde said.

"And didn't you see Aquero?"

"No, child." Aunt Bernarde, who had once wept through an unwanted pregnancy but was now respectably wed for the second time, looked down at her small relative. "You are the only one who sees anything at all."

"Nobody else sees anything at all," Madame Jacomet was informing her husband, as they sat at table the following Sunday.

"Then why do they go?" Inspector Jacomet took another mouthful of his wife's excellent coffee.

"The shoemaker's wife told Emma Estrade and Emma told me," Madame Jacomet said.

"Female gossip."

"There were forty or fifty people over at Massabielle this morning, all watching the little girl. The shoemaker's wife says she goes into a trance——"

"Who? Emma Estrade?"

"No, silly! The girl Soubirous. She becomes white as a candle, her eyes fixed, her lips moving as she utters a silent conversation."

"Now that is a miracle! A female having a silent conversation!"

"Oh, do listen! Emma Estrade thinks something ought to be done to stop it, or at least to find out what's going on. There's always the chance it could be the Virgin."

"The Virgin has been seen in most French villages at one time or other," the inspector said lazily. "You'd think she'd find somewhere else to land."

"The girl was down at the cave on Friday morning," his wife rushed on, "and yesterday she was there again. She said the lady had taught her a secret prayer for herself alone. And this morning there was quite a crowd there."

"Women," he scoffed.

"Doctor Douzous was there," she said triumphantly. "He went to see for himself and he was convinced that she really does see something. He stopped by to have a word with Emma and me, and he said it was an extraordinary thing to see. The girl looked like something from another world, but her pulse was quite steady and her breathing regular. He was very impressed."

"And what's the mysterious lady supposed to have said today?"

"The doctor asked the girl that and she answered, 'Aquero said to pray for sinners'. He wanted to ask her more but she went off to Confession."

"Very commendable," the inspector said dryly.

"The point is, what are you going to do about it?"

"A crowd of chattering women watching a girl saying her prayers is hardly a criminal offence," he protested mildly.

"But if you do nothing and the crowds get bigger and there's an accident, you'll never get your promotion."

"I remember the father," Jacomet said thoughtfully. "He did time for petty theft last year. I wonder if he's hit on a way of making a dishonest penny. I'll send Callet to pick up the girl and bring her back for questioning. You'd better step upstairs and ask Bernard Estrade to come down. I could do with an independent witness."

"I could stay," his wife said hopefully.

"You go and sit with Emma. We'll clear this up in an hour."

Inspector Jacomet stretched luxuriously, wondering if it were permissible to charge one's wife with nagging.

Two hours later he threw down his pen and scowled at the child seated at the other side of the desk. It was incredible but he had been quite unable to shake the girl's ridiculous story.

She had come quietly with the constable and curtsied politely. Jacomet couldn't recall having noticed her among the other children, and he studied her with particular attention. She was very tiny and very thin, he decided, and rather pale, but neat and clean, her skirt carefully patched, her dark hair looped tidily at the nape of her neck. Her eyes were fixed upon him unwaveringly which, he knew from experience, meant nothing. Some of the biggest rogues had the most innocent eyes. What did impress him was her tranquillity. She sat, without fidgeting, her hands folded in her lap, and answered his questions in a rapid, almost casual manner.

By the fire, Monsieur Estrade, who as tax collector, occupied a flat above the Inspector's, sat making careful notes.

Jacomet himself was making notes. A thin sheaf of them, the writing becoming wilder and larger as the interrogation proceeded, lay on the desk.

He had tried everything from promises of protection to verbal traps and threats of prison. The girl simply sat there, calmly correcting the deliberate errors he had made in the record of her replies, telling the same fantastic story. Yes, she was Bernadette Soubirous, aged fourteen. No, she couldn't read or write yet. Yes, she had been to Massabielle six times and each time Aquero had been there. No, she wasn't making anything up, or taking any money, or trying to cause a riot. Who was Aquero? Aquero was a very lovely little lady. Was Aquero real? More real than anything Bernadette had ever seen. Then why didn't other people see her? She couldn't understand that any more than the Inspector.

"So! we have a gloriously beautiful young lady who appears and vanishes, who climbs about with bare feet in the middle of February, whom nobody can see or hear except you! Your father's an unemployed layabout, your aunt keeps a tavern, and you can't even spell your own name but lovely ladies pop up out of caves to give Bernadette Soubirous private messages!"

"When you shake your head the tassel on your cap bobs up and down," Bernadette remarked with interest.

By the fire Estrade uttered a smothered sound which he turned hastily into a cough.

"That does it!" Jacomet slammed his fist, scattering the papers. "If you don't instantly confess, I'll put you in prison and throw away the key. Yes. What is it?"

"The girl's father is here," Constable Callet said.

"Tell him to take her home, and tell him from me that if she goes near Massabielle again, I'll lock up the whole Soubirous tribe!" the Inspector roared.

Bernadette, dismissed, took a last inquisitive look at the bobbing tassel and withdrew.

"And that," said Louise, unconsciously echoing Jacomet, "does it! We can't risk offending the police. You'll go straight to school tomorrow and you'll not go near Massabielle again."

"Aquero will miss me," Bernadette said sadly.

"She can miss you all she likes. You'll do as you're told," Louise snapped.

So it was really over. Now that the police were interested her parents would never allow the visits to continue. The beautiful little lady would wait in vain in the darkness of the cave. Mingled with the bitter disappointment was a thread of relief. It was not very pleasant to be followed about and questioned.

Louise escorted Bernadette to school herself the next morning, in case the child was tempted to disobey, but Bernadette went without argument. It was a clear day with a hint of sunshine, and Louise's own spirits rose. She was still cleaning at Madame Millet's twice a week and bringing back regular sums of money from the washing she had for other ladies. François had a part-time labouring job for a couple of weeks, and all the children were healthy. Even Bernadette's asthma seemed to be improving. When the odd events over at Massabielle were forgotten, they would all be back to normal.

The morning passed quietly. Bernadette made valiant and unavailing efforts to learn the first part of the Creed. It was strange but she could remember every word of the prayer Aquero had told her. She might never go to the cave again but she would say the prayer every day until she died. Her lips moved silently as she bent her head over the slate on which she had painstakingly chalked a wobbly B.

It was when she was returning to school in the afternoon

that the event she was never afterwards able to explain happened. She had reached the school gates when the air in front of her became as solid as wood. She could see nothing, but the barrier before her was impassable.

'I am really dreaming now,' she thought, 'and there isn't anything to see.'

Her outstretched hands beat against the invisible barrier, and then unseen hands were pushing her about, forcing her into the opposite direction, and she was running, as helplessly as a feather caught in the wind, back to the grotto.

Vaguely she could see figures scurrying alongside her. Two policemen were marching one each side of her, and she thought they were trying to ask questions, but their forms and voices were indistinct and she had no time to answer.

Aquero was waiting, and Aquero would be lonely if her friend wasn't there to meet her. For the first time Bernadette dimly understood that other people couldn't see Aquero not because she wasn't real, but because she was real in a different way. She was more intensely alive than anybody Bernadette had ever seen, but the life that was in her was not chained within flesh, even though she appeared quite solid. She had been flesh once, but now the force that moulded her was older than the beginning of time.

The cave, its narrow cleft at the side, yawned before her. Bernadette dropped to her knees and pulled out her rosary. She was very late but Aquero would understand and come as quickly as possible. She recited her prayers, only faintly aware of the other people who had drawn near, for her attention was concentrated upon the niche.

The niche remained empty. No sense in getting impatient. Aquero probably had other people to visit. She would come as soon as she could, and in the meantime one may as well recite another rosary.

A square face, bisected by a large moustache and surmounted by a cocked hat, loomed in front of her.

"Where's the lady then?"

Sergeant d'Angla enquired with genial ferocity.

"Scared of the police, is she?"

There were indignant hisses from the crowd.

Bernadette had completed her third rosary, and the niche was still empty. Perhaps Aquero was on the ledge at the back of the big cave. It was typical, Bernadette thought ruefully, of her own stupidity that she should wait outside when Aquero was probably inside the cave sheltering from the cold!

But the cave was empty too. The ledge was deserted, and the only sound was the crunching of pebbles under her wooden sabots.

She began to cry, tears sliding down her cheeks. She had been so certain but the lady hadn't come. Aquero had probably waited and waited, and in the end had given up and gone away again. The cave was empty and the crystal gone and only the clouds remained.

FOUR

"So, gentlemen, not only has it started up all over again, but you seem to have been affected by the prevailing madness," Inspector Jacomet said.

At the Cafe Francais a group of friends had gathered for the customary Wednesday night drink. Jacomet and his lodger, Bernard Estrade, occupied adjoining seats at the round table. Opposite them the lawyer, Dufo, sat stiffly like the retired officer he was. Dr Douzous leaned an elbow on the table and gazed thoughtfully into his goblet of brandy. At a little distance the Mayor, Monsieur Lacade, shared a narrower table with Monsieur Dutour, the Imperial Prosecutor.

"You need not trouble to include me in that remark," the Mayor observed. "I've not been near Massabielle and I wouldn't know the Soubirous child if I fell over her. What I do feel is that if we run around like chickens with their heads cut off we run the risk of blowing the whole affair up out of all proportion and making fools of ourselves into the bargain."

"No sense in being like ostriches and hiding our heads in the sand either," Jacomet said testily.

"The girl hasn't broken any laws," Dutour said. "Nobody can stop people saying their prayers. I agree there's always the danger of riot, but from everything I've heard these people arrive quietly, recite their rosaries and then go home again."

"D'Angla was certain it was all over on Monday," Jacomet said gloomily. "The lady didn't turn up as you know, and the girl went home in floods of tears. But there were more than a hundred people there on Tuesday morning—know I've no patience with superstition but I am interested in mental illness. It's becoming recognized that the mind exerts immense influence over the body."

There was a faint groan from one or two of the others who knew that it was difficult to get the doctor off his favourite hobby-horse.

"You saw the girl on three occasions," Lacade said. "What are your findings?"

"Inconclusive. Remember I've only seen her at the grotto, and on each occasion she was in ecstasy except at her arrival and departure, so it is hard to make a diagnosis."

"But your overall impression?"

"She's genuine and not play-acting," the doctor said. "These hallucinations occur only down at Massabielle. They are always the same, a young lady in white who recites the rosary. I would say incipient religious mania. The only trouble is that she shows none of the usual signs of mania. She neither twitches, nor rolls about on the ground, nor foams at the mouth. Therefore I say that a detailed medical examination is required."

"She's a religious fraud!" Jacomet exclaimed. "A quick-witted little actress."

"You were unable to get her to contradict herself, weren't you?" Dutour remarked slyly.

"If the girl suffers from delusions whenever she visits Massabielle, or if she is merely play-acting," Dufo mused, "how is it that she saw nothing on Monday? From all reports she was deeply distressed, so much so that her mother allowed her to resume her visits to the grotto."

"I can't explain everything," Jacomet said irritably. "Monsieur Estrade has not favoured us with his opinion," Dufo said.

"I believe that she sees a genuine vision," the Tax Inspector said briefly.

"As all visions originate in the diseased imaginations of the insane there can be no such thing as a genuine one," said the doctor.

"Look, I was quite certain when my sister first told me about it that the whole affair was a pack of nonsense!" Estrade said vigorously. "Yesterday morning my sister and her friend were intending to walk down to the cave at first light. I laughed at them. I reminded them the so-called vision had been conspicuously absent on Monday. And I considered myself to be at an advantage for I was present when our friend Jacomet questioned the girl. I told him then that in my opinion she was sincere but deluded."

"But you went to the grotto yesterday."

"To please the ladies. Anyway the forest lane is lonely, and I considered my sister and her friend needed an escort. I teased them as we went along, asking what they would do if the devil appeared to carry them off. There were about a hundred people there by the time the little girl came."

"And?" Dutour asked as the other paused.

"I cannot express it," Estrade said. "The girl arrived and knelt down with her rosary. She looked up at the cleft in the rock and her face gradually changed. It became luminous, almost transparent. Her eyes glowed. She was listening intently, and then her lips would move rapidly. The expression on her face changed from deep sadness to the most intense joy. I tell you that child was holding a conversation with something or somebody. After about an hour the look faded gradually and she rose."

"And what was this long conversation all about?" Dutour asked.

"A woman with her, one of her aunts, I think, asked her that. I heard the reply quite clearly. She said, 'Aquero gave me three secrets but they are only for me'."

"That won't please the clergy," Jacomet said dryly.
"They don't approve of private revelations."

"I believe," Estrade said solemnly, "that a daily miracle is taking place over at Massabielle. I can only urge you to go and see for yourself."

"You weren't there this morning."

"I do have work to do," Estrade said with dignity.

"I was there this morning," Dufo said.

"And were you equally impressed?" Lacade asked.

"I have been puzzling about it all day," the lawyer said slowly. "There were about two hundred people down at Massabielle this morning, but I got there early and had a close view. A lot of people had packed into the lower cave and some of them were clinging to the rocks at the side."

"I knew it—there'll be an accident and I'll be held responsible," Jacomet said gloomily.

"The girl arrived and went to what seems to be her usual place," Dufo continued. "She didn't seem to notice the crowd, but knelt down and took out her rosary. A woman nearby gave her a lighted candle to hold. A few minutes later her face changed just as Estrade has told you. I was very deeply moved, I admit, but I kept my critical faculties."

"Delighted to hear it," Jacomet muttered.

"I was watching the girl closely," Dufo said, "and quite suddenly her face was enveloped in a white cloud, a kind of vapour. It was so extraordinary that I could scarcely believe the evidence of my senses, but others saw it too and cried out."

"Where did the cloud come from?" Dutour asked.

"It sounds quite mad," Dufo apologized, "but it seemed to me that the mist came out of herself. Her face was hidden in it for about six or seven minutes, and yet there was a wind blowing. It blew the flame of her candle almost horizontal, until the fire was licking her forefinger but she never moved."

"And then?" Estrade was leaning forward tensely.

"The mist cleared and she jumped up and called out, 'who touched the rose bush?'"

"What bush is that?" Dutour wanted to know.

"A bush growing up the rock just below the cleft. Some boys were scrambling up it."

"Was that the end of it?" Jacomet asked, "or were there more signs and wonders?"

"She passed the candle to someone and then she knelt down and kissed the ground several times. She kept saying over and over, 'Penance'. Just that one word in a sad little voice. And then she crossed herself and stood up. She looked quite ordinary again."

"You're right," Lacade said briefly. "It is an extraordinary tale."

"There is one thing more," said Dufo. "She passed very close to me as she was leaving, and I caught hold of her hands. They were perfectly clear, no trace of a burn."

"A miracle," said Estrade.

"Miracle nothing!" the docter looked annoyed. "The phenomenon is well known in medical circles. It's a symptom of intense hysteria. All so-called stigmatics come into the same category."

"And the white cloud?"

"Now that I can't explain, but that doesn't mean there isn't an explanation."

"This talk of clouds and penance is all very well," Dutour said irritably, "but where does it leave us?"

"The local newspaper's got hold of the story," Jacomet said, "and that means it'll be syndicated at Pau and Tarbes."

"Can't the clergy do something to stop it? It seems to be more in their province," the mayor asked.

"I had a talk with L'Abbé Peyramale," Jacomet said. "I'm afraid we didn't get very far. He informs me that he has forbidden the curates to go near Massabielle and that he has no intention of going there himself. I pressed him for an opinion but he simply said that if a heavenly being was appearing at Massabielle she could continue to do so without any help from him."

"He's a wily old fox!" Dr Douzous exclaimed in amusement.

"I suggest," said Jacomet, "that we each of us send a report of this affair to our immediate superiors. Then, if it escalates, we can be seen to have been taking a very careful note of the proceedings. I myself will inform the Sub-Prefect at Argeles that I am of the opinion a very clever religious fraud is being perpetrated, but that the situation is under control. D'Angla has informed me he intends to send a similar report to his Lieutenant at Argeles."

"I will write to the Prefect of Tarbes," the mayor said. "Baron Massey is an excellent man, very reasonable and businesslike. If I were you, Dutour, I'd write to the Prosecutor General at Pau and ask him to clarify the legal position."

"And as you're all going to be so busy, my friends," said Estrade, draining his glass and rising, "I'll be off to my bed for a good night's sleep before I go to Massabielle at dawn."

It was, in fact, just before dawn when he and his sister scrambled the last few yards down the cliff to the cave below. With them was Elfrida Lacrampe, a young lady who, as daughter of a hotel owner, considered an early morning trip to watch a peasant child as something of a condescension on her own part. The place was already crowded though it was cold and rainy, with dark clouds tossing across the sky. Most people were sheltering in the lower cave, packed so closely that there was scarcely room to kneel, but others were perched on rocks the other side of the stream or were kneeling on the strip of sandy grass in front of the cliff.

The waiting seemed long. Grey dawn had broken when Bernadette, flanked by her Aunts Bernarde, Basile and Lucile came hurrying down the slope. Estrade was near enough to smile, but the girl was squeezing through the press of spectators and didn't seem to notice him.

So many people, she thought, irritably trying to force her way to her usual place. She was already late and dreaded having to keep Aquero waiting. If only they would have the manners to stand back a little!

Her place gained with difficulty she sank to her knees and pulled out her rosary. All around her people were taking out their own beads and trying to light their candles, but her own eyes were fixed on the niche.

The crystal blazed in the darkness of the rock and then dimmed to a golden glow as the little lady in the white dress came into focus. There was always the fear that she might not come, but the fear became relief as soon as the crystal began to glow. She recited the rosary slowly, noting how, as usual, Aquero slid the pearls of her own beads between finger and thumb without moving her lips.

The rosary finished, Bernadette put her own cheap string back in her pocket and prepared to enter into the deep and loving contemplation in which the rest of the world was blotted out.

Aquero, however, seemed brisk and authoritative this morning. Her voice, vibrating in the centre of Bernadette's forehead, was clear and decided.

"Go drink and wash at the spring."

The spring must mean the eddying of the little waves of the river where it joined the mill-stream. Moving on her knees over the wet ground Bernadette made her way rapidly along the strip of beach towards the water. Something was wrong. She glanced back and saw that Aquero was shaking her head. Perhaps she ought to be on her feet. Starting to rise she was sent back to her knees with a frown from the lady in the niche. So that wasn't right either. Aquero was pointing now within the lower cave. On her knees again, Bernadette changed direction and headed for the cave. She was aware of the people making way for her, but her attention was concentrated on Aquero. There were no springs inside the cave, only grass and rain-splashed pebbles.

Bernadette emerged again and looked up at Aquero helplessly. It was all very confusing but then she had evidently misunderstood. The slim white finger however still pointed within the cave. She heaved a sigh and set off again, her head bent to the ground.

A patch of muddy earth within the cave caught her eye. Some instinct told her that this was the spot, but her main feeling was one of dismay. She scooped a palmful of the earth up and threw it down, hating the wet, cloying stuff that stuck to her fingers and smelt foul. The hollow made by her hand was filling with dirty liquid. She scooped out two more handfuls of earth and then managed to retain a small quantity of the filthy water and drank it. It tasted so awful that her stomach heaved in protest.

Aquero had told her to wash her face in the spring. She had no idea why such an order had been given, but she did know that Aquero was to be obeyed. She rubbed some of the mud on to her cheeks and glanced hopefully towards the niche.

"Eat the plant growing there," Aquero said. There was nothing but the coarse grass. Bernadette pulled a handful and stuffed it into her mouth. Around her the people were shifting and muttering.

The grass tasted worse than the water. She chewed it and

managed to force some down, spitting out the rest. At least she had obeyed, and that was the important thing. She went rapidly on her knees to her place beneath the niche and looked up expectantly, but the cleft in the rock was empty.

"Child, what in the world has come over you?" Aunt Basile, scarlet with embarrassment was hauling her to her feet, rubbing at the mud with a corner of her shawl. "You must be out of your wits to go smearing your face with mud and eating grass."

The crowd was drifting away, many of them exclaiming angrily. Others were crowding about, asking questions, their expressions full of puzzled concern. She answered politely, but she was as puzzled as any of them.

Not that it made much difference, she decided, as they made their way in the rain back to the cachot. When Aquero gave an order it had to be obeyed for, young and fragile though the lady was, she was evidently accustomed to authority. If she had wished to give reasons she would have done so.

"Nobody will come to Massabielle if you behave like a little animal!" Aunt Lucile was scolding.

Bernadette looked at her in surprise, wondering why her aunt should be bothered about what the other people thought or whether they came or not.

At Massabielle, the scooped hollow of mud had filled and overflowed. The water, bubbling up strongly now, was threading its way across the floor of the lower cave.

"I don't understand it," Estrade said. "I don't understand how I could have been mistaken. I shall go to the cachot myself and find out what's going on."

"Why bother?" Elfrida Lacrampe shrugged elegant shoulders. "We've made fools of ourselves, that's all. The poor girl's unbalanced. I'm only sorry I got out of a nice, warm bed to come and watch a little lunatic."

"There's a lot of water splashing up out of where the girl drank," a small child remarked to nobody in particular.

The water fascinated her so much that she squatted down and dabbled her hand in it. In her pocket was a little jar in which she had meant to fish for tiddlers after the people had gone. She brought it out and dipped it into the little pool. It filled up with a little sucking sound, and she held it up to the greyish light and squinted at the blobs of reddish mud falling to the bottom and forming a thick sediment there.

Her father was at home that morning. He often stayed at home when his eye was paining him. He'd lost the sight of it many years before when he'd been working in the quarry and some blasting had gone wrong. The eye was still there but so badly scarred that Dr Douzous had said there was no possibility of his ever being able to see out of it again.

The child didn't know why she had suddenly thought of her father's eye, but she forgot about the tiddlers and set off home, carrying the jar of muddy water.

The rain eased off towards evening but the spring continued to bubble up out of the hollowed earth, flowing more strongly.

In the warm sitting-room of his handsome house Monsieur Dutour laid down his pen and scowled at the two figures standing in front of him. They had been standing there for over two hours and the woman looked ready to drop. He was sorry for her and inclined to believe that she wasn't a party to any fraud. Indeed he could have sworn that she was genuinely confused and upset. It was much more likely that her husband was behind it.

As for the girl! He had no idea what to make of her. She was small and thin and neat, and she'd gone along quite happily with the constable. Certainly she didn't look like the mud-smeared lunatic described to him by those who'd

c

been down at Massabielle that morning. She'd answered all his questions readily; she'd calmly corrected him when he'd tried Jacomet's trick of reading back to her false statements, and now she was actually beginning to answer him back.

"If the Inspector told you that I said I'd seen the Virgin he's wrong, sir!"

"But do you see her?"

"I see Aquero. I don't know her name."

"And Aquero tells you to eat grass like an animal?"

"You eat salad, sir," she retorted.

"Now don't get clever with me, young lady!" He rose, striking the desk with the flat of his hand.

"Oh, sir, she's not clever!" the mother cried out. "She's very simple and very good."

"I promised Aquero I'd go every day for fifteen days."

"And if you're put in prison, what will you do then?" he enquired.

"If I can't go, then I won't go," she told him.

At her side Louise was sobbing, bits of hair trailing from under her hood, her eyes red-rimmed and blurred. She had begun to sway slightly.

"There's a chair over there," he said impatiently. "You may sit down."

She collapsed into it, her hands to her face. Dutour turned to a side-table to pour himself some wine. A stiff brandy would have been more acceptable but his wife had run out of cognac. Over his shoulder he said to the girl, "You may as well sit down too."

The calm dark eyes that had gazed dreamily through him were looking at him now, and he was startled by the blazing contempt in them. He had never seen such a look in a child's eyes before.

"No, thank you," she said icily, "I might dirty the chair."

"Sit down!" he shouted.

Without removing her gaze she plonked herself cross-legged on the carpet.

The Imperial Prosecutor, looking down at the defiant figure with the blazing eyes, felt suddenly very small and very mean. He had always prided himself on his ability to trick confessions out of the accused but his talent seemed unworthy and his tactics cheap.

"All that I've written down," he said shrilly, "is what you have said to me."

"I told the truth," she said in the same icy tone, "and you have read out a lot of lies."

"Out!" Shaking with what he chose to believe was temper he threw down his pen and pointed to the door. "Get out, the pair of you! One more trip to the grotto and I'll have you in a cell!"

He was still shaking as they let themselves out into the street again.

Louise was still crying. She had been so frightened when the policeman came, and she was so tired and bewildered by all the strange things that were happening. Even Bernadette was becoming strange. She had been such a good, quiet girl, and now when she wasn't behaving like a maniac, or talking to someone nobody else could see, she was being rude to important officials.

"Couldn't you stay away from Massabielle just for tomorrow?" she pleaded.

But Bernadette only replied, "I'm sorry, maman, but I promised Aquero."

FIVE

L'Abbé Peyramale was in a bad humour. He had slept badly and he had a twinge of rheumatism, not enough to cripple him but enough to make him aware of the fact that he was past middle age and that spring had not yet come.

He had hoped for a peaceful and profitable year, but this business at Massabielle was upsetting everyone. Already that day he had sent away a group of silly females who had begged him to have a special Mass offered in honour of the lady.

"And I trust and pray the notion didn't originate with anybody here," he said sharply, sweeping a glare around his assembled curates.

"For my own part," L'Abbé Pomian said, "I am beginning to think the whole affair is a put-up job. I was impressed at first when she came and told me her story."

"And now?"

"If the visions are genuine, surely one would expect to find some improvement in her intelligence, some inclination towards sanctity. I'm afraid the Soubirous girl displays neither. She's still extremely backward and far from showing any inclination towards sanctity she's become quite naughty. She took a box of snuff to school with her yesterday and set the whole class sneezing. Sister Damian was very cross."

"A bit of childish mischief," L'Abbé Pene excused.

"I wish she'd confine herself to handing out snuff," L'Abbé Serras said. "That's surely harmless, but this grotesque play-acting in the grotto smacks of blasphemy to me. Crawling around and eating grass!"

"But the spring of water is increasing," L'Abbé Pene said. "I understand some workmen have dug a channel and sunk a basin for it to flow properly."

"There's no mystery about the spring," said L'Abbé Pomian. "A shepherd was telling me there's been a spring seen inside the cave before. It's been seen at irregular intervals for centuries—something to do with the level of the river."

"The vision didn't appear last Friday," L'Abbé Pene said. "I hear the child went there and said her prayers and walked about on her knees kissing the ground, but nothing happened and she went home in tears."

"Ah, that explains why she wasn't in school that day," L'Abbé Pomian said.

"From all accounts the vision was back on Saturday," L'Abbé Serras said grimly. "Monsieur Clarens told me there were six or seven hundred people there, and the girl was for more than an hour in ecstasy. He used that very word, 'ecstasy', though he did say that he considered there was some medical reason for it."

"And afterwards?"

"Apparently she got up quite calmly and went home. The same thing happened on Sunday morning, except that the crowds were bigger."

"I'm told they imitate her," L'Abbé Pomian said.

"They recite the rosary on their knees, and they kiss the ground when she kisses the ground. I spoke to her after High Mass on Sunday, and told her she was making a spectacle of herself, allowing the people to follow her about. She was quite impertinent in her answer. She said 'I don't ask them to come, and I can't stop them'."

"She could stop going herself," L'Abbé Serras said. "The whole thing would die a natural death then, but she was interrogated on Sunday evening by the Prosecutor General himself, and she was obdurate. Monsieur Dutour said they questioned her for over an hour. One of the Sisters went with her and the poor woman ended up in tears, but the Soubirous girl just went on saying the same things over and over again."

"And now she has started blessing rosaries," L'Abbé Pomian said.

"*What!*" L'Abbé Peyramale's massive grey head shot up. "Yesterday morning she had two rosaries with her. She held one up to the cleft in the rock and waved it about. A lot of those who were watching did the same thing. Elfrida Lacrampe had it from Madame Cazenave."

"We will have to do something," L'Abbé Pene said. "We cannot possibly rely on rumours. If the little girl is innocent of fraud she needs our protection. At the very least we must go down there and find out for ourselves."

L'Abbé Peyramale gazed at them for a moment in silence. Devout, earnest young priests, he thought, apt to gossip and jump to conclusions, but sincere and very conscientious.

"My prohibition still stands," he said at last. "We will not visit Massabielle or utter any opinion on the happenings there. We will simply wait and see. Now we all have our duties to perform, let us get to them."

He rose and went out into the garden, his Missal in his hand. The weather did seem a trifle milder. Perhaps after all, the sharp frost had not blighted his roses. They made a brave show in the summer time, a glory of velvet blossom and satin leaves. He opened his Missal and began to pace the path slowly, his head bent.

The crunching of wooden sabots on the gravel disturbed him. He looked up, frowning slightly for he disliked having his Office interrupted, and saw a small girl on the path before him. Nearer the gate and looking as if she were ready to take to her heels was a stout peasant woman.

"Yes?" He nodded curtly at the child.

"If you please, Father, I'd like a word."

The deep voice coming up from the tiny frame was startling. He narrowed his eyes more attentively at the round, pale face framed in a headscarf, the big dark eyes under strongly marked brows. An inkling as to who she might be broke upon him but he said gruffly, "Who are you and what do you want?"

"I'm Bernadette Soubirous, and that's my Aunt Basile over there."

"Ah, yes, you're the little liar who pretends to see a lady over at Massabielle."

"I do see her," Bernadette said simply.

"And now I hear you've been blessing rosaries!" he accused.

"I'm not a priest, so I couldn't do anything like that."

"You were waving a rosary above your head yesterday," he said coldly.

"Oh, that!" To his surprise she laughed, teeth small and white between her full lips. "Pauline Sans asked me to use her rosary at Massabielle yesterday and I said I would, but when Aquero came she asked me where my rosary was. I held up the one I was carrying to show her, and she looked across and said, 'Not that one. Use your own'. So I put it away and took out my own."

It sounded convincing as the girl told it.

Scowling, L'Abbé Peyramale said brusquely, "So, what do you want with me then?"

"At Massabielle this morning the lady gave me a message for you."

"Did she indeed? Well, you'd better deliver it then."

Bernadette squeezed her eyes shut for a moment and then repeated docilely. "Aquero said, 'Go tell the priests I want a chapel built here'."

"And that just shows your foolishness in making up such a tale," Peyramale said. "Even if I wished, and I don't wish, I've no authority to build chapels. You should have been sent to the Bishop of Tarbes with a message like that."

"But I don't know the Bishop," the child said sensibly.

"Even if you did he'd require the permission of the Minister of Works."

"I don't know him either," she said, biting her lip anxiously.

"Then you'll have to go back and tell her you've failed, won't you?" Peyramale said.

"Couldn't you put a word in to the gentleman?" she suggested.

"To have a chapel built at the behest of an invisible woman who climbs round caves in her bare feet! Who is this woman anyway? What's her name?"

"I call her Aquero."

" 'Aquero' means 'Thing' which is no name at all! What does she call herself?"

"She doesn't call herself anything, Father."

"Then you'd better go back and ask her," Peyramale said loudly. "Oh, and has she any money?"

"I don't think so, Father."

"Neither have I," said Peyramale. "So you'd better go back and tell this nameless, penniless lady that I don't take messages from folk I don't know."

"She'll be very disappointed," Bernadette pleaded.

"I can't help that!" Goaded by a consciousness that he was yielding to the charm of the big eyes and the husky voice, Peyramale took refuge in bluster. "You can go away and tell Aquero that L'Abbé Peyramale doesn't accept messages from nameless females. She's to give her name and then *I'll* decide about the value of the messages she sends.

Go and tell her that!"

He had overdone the ferocity of his manner. Bernadette took one terrified glance at his face and clattered through the gate.

"Never again," moaned Aunt Basile through chattering teeth, "will I face L'Abbé Peyramale! I was so frightened that my knees shook. You put him in a fearful rage!"

"It was very good of you to come with me," Bernadette said gratefully.

Her own knees were trembling and her heart hammering. She'd only seen the priest before from a distance in the pulpit, but close to he was even more frightening. It had taken her nearly all day to pluck up sufficient courage to approach the presbytery, and the bulky figure in the black cassock with the fierce voice had shaken her much more than the three police officials who had questioned her. Policemen could only put you in prison and sooner or later they let you out again, but the parish priest could threaten hell itself and, according to Aunt Bernarde, was quite capable of sending people there.

It was then, with a shock of dismay, that realized she had neglected to give L'Abbé Peyramale all the message.

His Office recited, he was back in his sitting-room, drafting a letter to the Bishop of Tarbes who had requested that he be kept informed of the progress of events. As he made notes Peyramale hoped devoutly that any further progress would stop.

Lourdes was a pleasant, sleepy town with a sprinkling of gentry to leaven the great mass of peasant farmers and artisans. There was still too much poverty and illiteracy, and the rate of child mortality was appalling, but the officials on the Medical Board were working hard to eradicate such evils. 'And I,' thought Peyramale, 'am working to eradicate other kinds of evil.' Fraud, idolatry, superstition, all those relics of the Middle Ages were a bar to the propagation of the Faith. Since the crowning of the Emperor an uneasy peace existed between Church and State, but the shadow of Voltaire's rationalism still hung over France, and any attempts to bring back miracles and visions could only drag religion into disrepute.

"If you please, Father." He glanced up as his housekeeper came in.

"Yes, Dominiquette?"

"The Soubirous child is here again," Dominiquette said. "She's by herself and very nervous."

"But not so nervous that she doesn't come sneaking back!"

"She says she forgot to give you part of the message, Father. I do wish you would see her for a few minutes."

"I don't see why I should waste my time," he retorted, but he was already making signs to her to open the door.

Bernadette inserted herself through the opening in bits. That was the only way he could think of to describe the manner in which first her head, then her arm, and then the rest of her came into view. Behind her, a mulish expression on his face, came L'Abbé Pene.

"You'd better stay," Peyramale said, anticipating the request.

"Thank you, Father." The young curate seated himself in one of the high-back chairs and looked attentively at the child.

His superior was also watching her. She looked, as Dominiquette had said, exceedingly nervous, but she also looked wrought up to a pitch of excited endurance that might very well end in hysterical tears.

"So you're back, are you? And what new fantasy have you got this time?" he enquired sarcastically.

"I forgot to give you the rest of Aquero's message," she

said nervously.

"She's already asked for a chapel," he said coldly. "Don't tell me she wants more!"

"Aquero said, 'Go tell the priests I want a chapel built here and I want people to come here in processions'."

"Processions as well as a chapel! She's getting ambitious," Peyramale observed.

"This lady of yours," L'Abbé Pene said gently. "Are you sure you see her?"

"As clear as I see you, Father."

"Then how is it that nobody else does?" snapped Peyramale.

"I don't know. She's there for anybody to see."

"And you've seen her—how many times? Eleven? Twelve?"

"About thirteen times, Father." She was counting silently on her fingers.

"And she's given you private messages?"

"Three of them."

"And the message for the priests."

"Yes, Father."

She was regaining her assurance a little.

"And she's beautiful? As beautiful as the statue in church?"

"She's better looking than that," Bernadette said promptly. "Anyway, the statue is a dead thing. Aquero is alive."

"How do you know?" he shot at her.

"She breathes and talks, and laughs, and moves around. She's a live lady."

"Whom nobody else has ever seen or heard! What makes you so special?"

"I don't know, Father. Perhaps I was the only one around on the first day she came to Massabielle."

"But there have been others since, and they see nothing.

Neither do they hear anything. Can you explain that?"

She shook her head.

"L'Abbé Pomian tells me you are a very ignorant girl."

"Yes, Father, I am," she agreed.

"You can't read or write. You only speak a few words of French. You can't even remember your Catechism properly."

"I'm sure she tries very hard," L'Abbé Pene excused.

"I do try," she agreed, "but it is useless. I'm too thick headed to learn much."

"And yet Aquero comes and gives you messages? Do you know it's a sin to tell lies?"

She nodded gravely.

"And do you know what a sinner is?" he persisted.

"Someone who loves sin," she said at once.

"That was a good answer," the curate said in a low voice.

"You had better think very carefully," Peyramale said sternly. "I don't believe in your story for a moment. Make no mistake about that! But if you persist in what you say, then you can take a message back."

"I'm to ask Aquero her name. I remembered that," she said proudly.

"You can add something to that." He rose and stared through the window at the bleak garden. "I understand there's a wild rose bush at Massabielle," he said.

"Under the cleft where Aquero stands," she agreed.

"Tell Aquero that if she wants a chapel and processions she's to give her name, and she's to make the rose-tree at Massabielle bloom. Do you understand that?"

"She's to give her name and make the rose-tree bloom," she repeated obediently.

"And now you can stop wasting my time and get out." He sat down again at his desk and picked up a pen.

Bernadette lingered, rubbing her nose with her forefinger.

"Was there something else?" He drew his eyebrows together into a frown.

"I was wondering," she said timidly, "if you could possibly run to a very small chapel? It would please Aquero."

The priest's scowl darkened, the veins on his forehead bulging.

"Well, perhaps later," she said, and was through the door again.

"What was it you called her?" Peyramale asked his curate. "A modest, gentle girl? She's more nerve than a wagonload of monkeys!"

"She has courage."

"Courage to face her parish priest with a catalogue of lies!"

"But the story she tells is such an unusual one," the curate protested.

"My dear fellow, there is nothing the least unusual about it," L'Abbé Peyramale said pityingly. "Young girls have been seeing lovely ladies in caves and discovering secret springs since the beginning of history. Yes, my friend, even in pre-Christian times! The name changes but the vision remains the same."

"Then do you think she's genuine?"

"I think it's possible. I also think it's possible that she's lying through her teeth."

"But if the rose-bush blooms," the curate said eagerly, "then we can be sure that the girl is truly seeing the Holy Virgin."

"If the rose-bush blooms, then the one thing of which we can be certain is that the girl does *not* see the Holy Virgin," said L'Abbé Peyramale.

"But only the Holy Virgin could make a rose-bush bloom at the beginning of March."

"And the Holy Virgin does not take orders from the

parish priest of a very obscure provincial town. If the tree blooms you can be sure there's fraud involved."

"So if it doesn't bloom?"

"Then we have excluded the possibility of organized fraud. I doubt if that girl or her family know anything about forced germination. That leaves four possibilities."

"Four?" L'Abbé looked confused.

"The girl may be merely play-acting in which case she requires a good spanking. She may be mentally disturbed in which case she needs skilled treatment. What remains is the supernatural, and as priests we both know there are two sides to that. The devil has his emissaries even in the mid-nineteenth century. In fact I am inclined to believe that he is more active these days than any previous time in history."

"And if it is—the other side?"

The curate leaned forward eagerly in his chair.

"If it is?" L'Abbé Peyramale laid down his pen and rose again. "If it is then the lady will announce her name, miracles will take place, chapels will be built, and a lot of people will make a lot of profit."

"And the Soubirous child?"

"Will never know what it is to be a child again. Yes, Dominiquette, what is it now?"

"I've just heard from the doctor's housekeeper, Father," she said, "that one of the quarry workers, Louis Bouriette, has regained the sight of an eye that was blinded years ago. He was in the surgery this afternoon, she says, and Dr Douzous can't understand it because, although the injury is still there, he can see out of the eye. He was telling the doctor that his youngest girl took a jar of the muddy water back from Massabielle, and he's been bathing his eye in it ever since."

"Thank you, Dominiquette," L'Abbé Peyramale said

gloomily.

"Don't you think it's good news, Father?" she asked in surprise.

"For Louis Bouriette," he answered curtly. "For the rest of us, I'm not so certain! No doubt every fool will shout 'miracle'. I'm not certain what a miracle is, or if it has anything to do with God at all. All that I am certain of is that I wouldn't like my hat to know what my head is thinking!"

SIX

It was the last day of the fifteen promised days. That was Bernadette's first thought when she woke that morning. On the previous day Aquero had not come in the morning, but after school there had been the familiar tugging sensation that drew her back to Massabielle, and Aquero had come. She had given no explanation for her morning's absence, but then Aquero came and went, not as she pleased, but in obedience to some great law. That much Bernadette understood.

She silently repeated the secret prayer Aquero had taught her, and moving quietly so as not to disturb Toinette, slid from under the blankets and began to dress. Her blouse and skirt had been washed the day before and her white stockings darned. Her toes curled shudderingly on the bare stone of the floor.

"Is it time to go?" Louise had woken up too and was quietly dressing.

"It's still early, maman, but I slept in bits all night," Bernadette whispered.

"Your father'll be awake soon." Louise glanced at the humped figure shrouded under the blanket. François was working regularly now and the moods of black depression were growing fewer. She had feared that these strange events would upset him, but he seemed quite proud of Bernadette and had been down to Massabielle several times when he had embarrassed her a little by informing everybody within earshot who he was. For her own part Louise was very happy to remain unknown.

By the time she had brushed her daughter's hair and secured it under the red kerchief the others were awake.

Toinette and the little boys went regularly to the grotto. The girl was puzzled and a little jealous, but seven-year-old Jean and three-year-old Justin enjoyed watching all the people and basked a little in the reflected glory.

Bernadette, her face washed and her shawl crossed neatly in front and knotted at her waist behind sat on the window-sill looking through the bars at the yard. It was too dark to see anything clearly but in the room Louise had kindled a small fire and lit two candles.

She was folding up the bedclothes now and Toinette was scrubbing Justin's face. Later on, when they returned from Massabielle and before the girls went to school, they would come back to eat the onion soup she had hung over the dancing flames. There was nothing, thought Bernadette, so tasty as a bowl of her mother's good onion soup with bits of white bread soaked in red wine floating in it.

Louise was talking to some people at the door. Her voice when she spoke to Bernadette was flustered.

"These gentlemen are doctors. They would like a few words with you."

Their top hats and cloaks made sweeping shadows on the wall. Bernadette curtsied politely, wishing they had not come. She was becoming accustomed to questions, but it was distracting to have to receive strangers just before she went to the grotto.

"So you are Bernadette Soubirous? Do you know how old you are, child?"

"Yes, sir." She looked at the tallest of the trio in faint surprise. "I'm fourteen, sir."

"And can you tell me the date?"

"It's Thursday, sir, early in March."

"And the year?"

"Eighteen fifty-eight, sir."

"How many fingers am I holding up?" one of them asked.

"Three, sir." She glanced past with questioning brows to where her mother stood, but Louise shrugged her shoulders.

"Do you know, Bernadette, who sits upon the throne?"

"The Emperor, sir."

"How many are two multiplied by three?"

"Six, I think," she said slowly.

"And eleven multiplied by seventeen?" he enquired.

"I don't know," she said in bewilderment.

"Fourteen multiplied by twenty-three?"

"I don't know that either," she said blankly. "What is it?"

"She has you there, Henri," one of the men said, laughing.

"Can you read, Bernadette?"

She shook her head.

"Can you tell me where Paris is?" another of them asked.

"In the north of the land, I think."

"Do you get headaches?"

"No, sir. I have chest aches when my asthma comes, but my head doesn't ache."

"She looks frail," one of them muttered.

"Can you remember what you had to eat yesterday?"

"Onion soup with bits of white bread in it for breakfast, a piece of cheese and some olives for my dinner, and cabbage with some maize bread for supper."

"You remembered that very well," one of the doctors said.

"We have the same things nearly every day, sir."

"But since you have been seeing the lady you've had other things to eat, haven't you? Nicer meals that kind people have given you?"

"I had a good dinner and a good supper when I stayed with Madame Millet, and Madame Nicolau gave me an orange the day before yesterday, and Monsieur Sajous asked me to have a bite with his family on Monday. I had a nice bit of cod."

"Very soon there'll be many people wanting to entertain you to dinner," the tallest gentleman said. "You may end up very rich indeed. Would you like to be very rich?"

"I don't think so, sir."

"How many times have you seen the lady?"

"About fourteen times."

"Are you sure it wasn't a light?"

"There is a light, sir, but Aquero appears in the midst of the light."

"You say she speaks in patois? How does she speak it?"

"Better than you do, sir!" Her temper was beginning to rise.

"But you are learning French, are you not?"

"I'm trying to learn, but it's very hard," she said dolefully.

"Then you're not clever?"

"Goodness, no!" she exclaimed.

"And yet the lady comes to you. Now why should she do that?"

"I don't know, sir. She hasn't told me yet."

"And you're expecting to see her again this morning?"

"I'm going to Massabielle after I've been to church."

"And the lady will come?"

"I'm hoping so, sir."

"Do you get flashes of light before your eyes?"

She shook her head, fidgeting a little.

"It's very puzzling," the tall gentleman said. "No trace of any hereditary mania, I suppose?"

"None, according to all reports. And no visual disturbance either, though it's hard to tell without examination. I would say 'impressionable', wouldn't you?"

"And an adolescent! One is reminded of Jeanne d'Arc at the same age. Have you heard of her, Bernadette?"

"Sister Damian told us a story about her," she nodded. "She saw angels. Do you think that was true?"

"I can't tell you, I wasn't there."

"And do you think——" he began, but she interrupted firmly, "I have to go, sir. The bell is ringing, so that we'll have to run to Mass."

"And what would you do if I told you that we'll have to send in a report saying we don't believe a word of what you've been saying?"

"Aquero told me to tell the truth, but she didn't say I had to make anybody believe it," Bernadette said calmly. "We have to go now. Jean, what are you doing?"

Jean, in the act of pocketing a silver coin tendered by one of the doctors, stopped short, his mouth half-open. The next instant his sister had pounced on him, turning out the lining of both his pockets, and was boxing his ears. Slightly breathless after her exertions she picked up the coin and gave it firmly back, her voice apologetic.

"My brother's very little and he doesn't understand."

"Didn't Aquero teach you not to turn down the chance of making a quick profit then?" the tall man asked, winking at his companions.

"No, and she didn't teach me how to laugh at the poor either," she said coldly, and clattered down the short passage to the street beyond.

The church was packed. She had never seen so many people at Mass on a weekday before. There were a few of the gentry there too, ladies in billowing crinolines and fur wraps, gentlemen in silk hats.

Her cousin, Jeanne Vedere, was kneeling next to her. Bernadette, shuffling sideways to make room for her, caught the urgent whisper, "Can I stay with you while the lady's there?"

"Right next to me," Bernadette whispered back.

"Cross your heart and cut your throat?"

"Cross my heart and cut my throat. Be quiet now. Sister is looking at us."

Jeanne subsided, assuming an expression of anguished piety.

It was past seven when they came out of church, and a grey dawn was breaking over the rooftops. Bernadette patiently submitted to Louise's fussy rearranging of the white capulet she wore, accepted the holy candle her aunt was pressing into her hand, and set off as quickly as she could with her relatives and neighbours crowding around.

It was with a little shock of excited anticipation that, as she hurried along the forest road, she heard the buzzing of many voices through the trees, and individual shouts of "Here she comes!" "She's here!" Aquero must have shown herself to all the people this morning. Now they would stop following Bernadette around and asking her foolish questions.

The cleft in the rock was still empty however. She hesitated for a moment, confused by the sea of faces and then she was caught up in the crowds as they surged forward.

"Let her pass! Let my little girl pass!" François was shouting, but his voice was drowned in the general chatter. Two soldiers had drawn their swords and were forcing a passage for her. When she had reached her usual place she looked round anxiously but Jeanne had vanished.

"Captain!" She tugged at the soldier's coat. "My cousin is here and I promised she could stay close. Can you find her? She's called Jeanne Vedere and she has a blue ribbon in her hair."

"Twenty thousand people here and she wants one with a blue ribbon in her hair! All right, missy. We'll find your cousin!"

The people, incredibly, were quietening down, dropping

to their knees. Among them at a few yards distance, a girl with a blue ribbon tying up her hair was waving her arm. The soldier, astonishment lengthening his face, strode towards her.

Monsieur Estrade, from his place on top of the cliff, had sacrificed his dignity in order to lie prone and peer over the edge. From this vantage point he could see the dark hollow of the cave with the bare and thorny branches of the rose tree clinging around it. On the ground beneath among the upturned faces he could see Bernadette's very clearly. It was impossible to mistake the translucent joy on her face. Her lips moved rapidly and then were closed firmly as she nodded her head, listening intently. Her smile was brilliant, as if a candle had been lighted behind her eyes, but a moment later sadness would veil the pleasure and tears would roll down her face. At her elbow knelt Inspector Jacomet, carefully taking notes in a little red notebook.

The look on the girl's face was fading. It was fully daylight now, and she had been less than twenty minutes on her knees. There were murmurs of disappointment from the crowd. Nothing had happened after all. The lady had shown herself only to the Soubirous girl, and the rose-tree had remained obstinately bare.

"Which proves this is not organized fraud," L'Abbé Peyramale said.

"Then the girl really sees something?" L'Abbé Pene looked hopeful.

"She believes she sees something," Peyramale corrected, "or she pretends she sees something. I cannot make up my mind which it is. What did the doctors from Bordeaux say?"

"That the child is backward intellectually but potentially intelligent, that she is impressionable and may have mistaken a gleam of sunlight on the side of the rock for a vision."

"Then why didn't everybody else see the light? No, what the good doctors mean is that they can't make a diagnosis! L'Abbé Pomian, would you call the Soubirous girl a lunatic?"

"No, indeed. Very stupid, but not insane. She gives quite sharp answers sometimes if her temper is roused. She does have a temper."

"Show me a girl worth her salt without a temper. She lacks training and education, but the intelligence is there."

"It might be cunning," L'Abbé Serras said.

"She answers so frankly, so openly," L'Abbé Rene said.

"Sister Theresa caught her smacking her sister in the playground," L'Abbé Pomian said.

"Did you imagine that a child who sees a vision stops behaving like a child?" Peyramale asked testily. "Well, Monsieur Estrade, you were there. What do you say?"

"When she rubbed that dirty mud on her face and chewed grass, I doubted. I admit it freely," Estrade said. "But now I no longer doubt. That spring she hollowed out flows like a torrent now."

"Those rocks are honeycombed with streams and pools," Pomian said. "And several elderly people have told me they've heard before of a stream at Massabielle."

"Cures are taking place," Estrade said. "Like the blind girl this morning who cried out that she was cured. It turned out she'd never been blind at all!"

"But Bouriette's eye *was* injured, and now he can see clearly out of it. And there are rumours of other inexplicable cures."

"Fortunately Holy Mother Church doesn't deal in rumours," Peyramale said dryly.

"But if the Blessed Virgin is coming to Lourdes——"

"She hasn't informed me of the fact. And she hasn't seen fit to give her name yet."

"Then you think she will?"

"Oh, I'm fairly certain, if there is anything beyond the naughtiness of a child in this, that the lady will come back and announce herself as 'Our Lady of the Caves', or 'Virgin of Peasants' or some such title," Peyramale said. "These visions usually follow a pattern."

"You sound as if you don't believe in any of them!" L'Abbé Rene stared at his superior in dismay.

"I believe that the Creator never breaks His own laws," Peyramale said. "If there are people who can transcend physical senses and attune themselves to the vibrations of a higher, spiritual reality, then those people have the genius of sanctity in them. They leave the earth while they are still on the earth and enter into a communion with worlds at which we can only guess. And these are the chosen of God."

"Then it doesn't sound much like poor little Bernadette Soubirous," L'Abbé Pene said regretfully.

"You think not?" The priest regarded him quizzically for an instant. "Ah, well, time will tell. At least there were no accidents this morning, so we may regard that as a small mercy. I shall write to His Lordship the Bishop this evening and tell him that the fifteen days are up, and I foresee no further disturbances."

At the Café Française the Mayor sipped an aperitif and raised his glass to his companions.

"My congratulations on the way in which you handled this morning, gentlemen. I expected a riot at least, especially after the rose-tree didn't bloom."

"I had my constable inside the grotto all night to obviate the possibility of a trick," Jacomet said.

"Very sensible, and the reinforcements kept the crowd under control. Have you done anything further?"

"I've put a watch on the Soubirous house," Dutour said. "We'll take note of everyone who goes in and out. If the parents accept money or gifts I'm confident we can secure a conviction for fraud."

"I've put a watch on the girl herself," Jacomet said grimly. "From now on she'll have a daily shadow to report if she even sneezes!"

"And I," said Lacade, with a faint air of triumph, "have had a sample of the water at Massabielle sent to Paris for analysis."

"You believe these tales of cures then!" Jacomet exclaimed.

"I believe it's possible the water has curative properties," the Mayor said. "The spas at Cauterets are not far distant."

"And we all know how prosperous the town of Cauterets is," Dutour said slyly.

"Lourdes could have become a very prosperous spa, if the water contained the required minerals in sufficient quantities," Lacade argued. "The proposed railway lines could be brought through Lourdes. As it is at the moment the proposed line from Paris bypasses us altogether."

"It would bring work to the town," Jacomet agreed. "And cut the crime rate," Dutour added.

"Funny thing that!" The Inspector looked thoughtful, "I was checking the books yesterday and since this business at Massabielle started not a single crime appears to have been committed in the district. At least there haven't been any arrests, but one usually pulls in a few drunks or gets the odd pickpocket. But there's been absolutely nothing."

"Coincidence," said Dutour.

"As you say," Jacomet agreed, "but I don't like it. It's not natural for no crimes to be committed."

"Hold your gaol for the Soubirous tribe," Dutour advised. "If you watch them closely you might be able to pull in the lot."

In the crowded classroom Sister Damian looked searchingly round the assembled class. The girls were restless this morning, most of them having been up before dawn. Bernadette, she saw, was in her usual place, wearing the look of frowning concentration that meant she was not following a word of the lesson. The girl looked tired and her breathing was harsh.

"Soubirous!"

"Yes, Sister Damian."

"I have a glass of water with some brown sugar in it on the table. You may pour yourself a small drink of it for your cough. We cannot have you disturbing the rest of the class."

"Thank you, Sister!"

Looking surprised and pleased the girl went to the table.

Watching her as she drank the nun said abruptly. "So it's over now, is it? No more lady?"

"I don't know, Sister. Aquero didn't say goodbye, so I shall go to the grotto now and then to see if she comes back," Bernadette said.

"You'll wait for an illusion?"

"No, Sister, I'll wait for Aquero. She may come back."

"Perhaps next time it'll be to see another child," Sister Damian said.

"It might be," Bernadette agreed.

"Even so, you must feel rather special to have been chosen first? Why do you think you were chosen?"

"There wasn't anybody better around at the time, I suppose."

"And you still don't know her name?"

"No, Sister."

"Bernadette, I wish you would think carefully," Sister Damian pleaded. "It's so easy to begin something and so very difficult to stop it. You're fourteen now and you won't stay a child for very much longer. What sort of life will you have when all this is over?"

"I don't know, Sister."

"But when you're grown up, what do you want to do? There must be ambition in you somewhere, something you want."

"Oh, yes!" Bernadette's face had brightened. "I'd like a corset with bones in it, the sort that makes you look bigger on top. Maman saw one at Madame Millet's, and she says they're all the rage in Paris!"

SEVEN

Monsieur Dutour and Inspector Jacomet stood just outside the cave and stared gloomily first at its interior and then at each other. It was impossible to miss the spring of water that jetted up strongly out of the ground and flowed in an unending stream down the makeshift channel into the sunken basin of stone. The basin itself overflowed and those who couldn't get near the source were washing themselves and filling a variety of jars and bottles from the splashing water. It ran clear now, throwing drops of crystal up to the dark stone and the clouded sky. Others were lighting candles and sticking them upright in the earth. Within the lower cave somebody—Jacomet wished he could get his hands on them—had set up a wire frame decorated with paper roses in which a plaster Madonna was insecurely fixed.

"And Lacade says it is ordinary drinking water after all," Dutour said. "The chemists in Paris were unanimous in the report. It is ordinary water."

"But the people still come," Jacomet said disapprovingly. "More and more of them come every day. Carriages are rolling in and whole families coming down from the valleys in farm-carts, on horseback, and on foot. They leave money here too."

"Who gets that?" Dutour asked sharply.

"I made enquiries," Jacomet assured him. "The money was collected by the schoolteacher and taken to L'Abbe Peyramale."

"Ah, ha!"

"Who ordered him to take it to the local almshouse where

it will be used to benefit the poor." Jacomet looked discouraged.

"What makes it so odd is that the Soubirous girl hasn't been near Massabielle for the last three weeks," Dutour said. "She goes to school every day, she answers questions, and kisses babies when silly mothers ask her to do so, but she hasn't been near the grotto."

"I know. I asked her myself why she hadn't been," Jacomet said, "and she shrugged her shoulders and said she hadn't felt like it."

"She won't accept any money or any presents," Dutour fretted. "She says nothing about anything that's happened and then she gives a brief answer and carries on with what she's doing. Sergeant d'Angla's wife went to see her and tried to slip a little something into her hand, and the girl jumped away as if she'd been stung. So what's she after?"

"I'm beginning to think she's genuinely deluded," Jacomet said. "What's more I think she's beginning to realize the fact herself, which is why she hasn't been here. After all the lady didn't give her name and the rose-tree didn't burst into flower, and that wretched spring has been seen before in the cave, and half the cures seem to be downright suspect and yet the people still come."

"Pray for rain tonight," Dutour advised. "It's the Feast of the Annunciation tomorrow, so if the crowds get any thicker and the lady turns up again!" He spread his hands wide.

"Monsieur Dufo and Estrade are both completely won over," said Jacomet. "They've been bowled over by that innocent smile and those big brown eyes. Fortunately you and I have interrogated too many rogues to be swept off our feet! Not that I would condemn her outright, mind! I'm truly beginning to think she may be suffering from some kind of mania."

"Dr Douzous doesn't think so."

"Dr. Douzous is never of the same opinion for an hour together," Jacomet scorned. "He fancies himself as the man of science, but he's half inclined to believe in all this superstitious nonsense!"

"And meanwhile the Church stands aloof, knowing very well that the priests will get the credit in the end, while you and I have to make ourselves unpopular by discrediting the whole affair."

"We don't seem to be doing terribly well at it," Jacomet murmured.

Overhead there was a low rumble of thunder and a few drops of rain spattered them.

At the cachot Bernadette lay, early the next morning, listening to the beating of the rain on the window. The family slept around her, her father's snores mingling with Justin's baby mutterings. When she thought of her family a feeling of sadness overwhelmed her. She had been so eager to return from Bartres, and she had imagined at the time that the tugging inside her had meant her parents needed her. Now she was aware it was Aquero who summoned her, and since the day she had gone to Massabielle to gather wood she seemed to have grown away from her family. The quiet rhythm of their lives had been interrupted by doctors, policemen, journalists and dozens of people whom she had never seen in her life before. Some of them called her a little cheat and threatened to lock her up, and some of them called her a little saint and so wanted to kiss her, and they all asked questions. She couldn't understand why they needed to ask so many questions when all they had to do was to clear the clouds from their eyes and see Aquero standing there. And all the time her parents kept looking at her as if they didn't know her, and she could feel a barrier growing, slowly and surely, between herself and those she loved most.

Aquero was coming! Every other thought fled before that realization as she sat bolt upright. Aquero was coming and she had to get up and go to the grotto. She was out of bed, shaking Louise by the shoulder, her voice an urgent whisper.

"Maman! Maman, get up! We have to go to Massabielle!" "Now? This minute?" Louise was struggling out of sleep.

"This minute! I feel it here!" Bernadette held her clenched fist to her solar plexus.

"François! François, get up!" Louise poked him energetically. "We're going to Massabielle."

"Oh, no! In an hour or two," François groaned.

"Right now. Bernadette says Aquero wants it!"

François rolled over to the side and groped for his trousers. He had always been a tolerant, easy-going man, leaving discipline to Louise, but he'd been working regularly for nearly a month now and a working man needed his sleep. Reaching for his jacket and beret he couldn't help wishing that Aquero chose more convenient times.

"Oh, do hurry!" Bernadette pleaded, as Louise hauled Toinette to her feet and gave her a slap to wake her up. "Do hurry!"

They hurried through the dark and dripping streets, their sabots clattering on the cobbles. At Aunt Bernarde's tavern there was a further delay while they knocked at the door, but the three aunts came tumbling out, tucking night-plaited hair under their kerchiefs, rubbing sleep from their eyes, anxiously checking rosaries and holy candles.

The path down the side of the cliff was slippery with mud, but Bernadette winged down it like a bird. Early as it was there were a few people already there, wandering up and down the little strip of beach, huddled under large umbrellas as they filled their water bottles at the spring.

Bernadette saw only that Aquero was already there. She stood in the niche within the glowing crystal and every part of her was more alive and more beautiful than anything the girl had ever seen.

She began to stammer an apology, but Aquero cut her short with a smiling shake of the head, and held up the long rosary of gold and pearls. The prayers must be said before the conversation could begin.

The rosary recited, Aquero made her great sweeping sign of the cross that hung golden on the air, and beckoned with one slender finger. She was moving away from the outer niche, retreating within the rock that twisted down to the ledge at the back of the big cave.

Bernadette moved rapidly on her knees into the cave. It was faintly illumined by the candles stuck into the ground, and a few sequins glittered from the hearts of the paper roses that crowned the plaster Madonna.

Aquero stood on the ledge, her blue eyes moving slowly around. There were several people on their knees near the spring and the Soubirous women had crowded behind. Aquero was looking at the makeshift altar of wire with its wobbly statue, and she seemed pleased, for she was bowing deeply to the others in the cave as if she were thanking them.

She had turned again to Bernadette, her head slightly inclined, as the girl spoke. There was so much to tell her that the words tumbled out helter-skelter, but Aquero never lost her expression of deep interest even in the smallest details of life at the cachot.

She was smiling still as Bernadette paused for breath, and into her smile had crept a hint of teasing. "If you please," Bernadette said, emboldened by the smile, "would you tell me your name?"

She had asked before and always been answered by a laughing shake of the head. On this occasion Aquero merely smiled.

"If you would tell me your name?" Bernadette tried again hopefully.

The smile had faded a little but there was encouragement in Aquero's expression, and she was no longer on the ledge but on the floor of the cave itself.

"Please, won't you let me know your name?" Bernadette pleaded.

Aquero was moving nearer. In a moment the radiance in which she moved would envelop them both, but a gulf yawned between them, an abyss of darkness and despair, and Aquero bore a look of anguish as if in her all the sorrows of the world had origin and end.

"Oh, please, Miss, won't you have the goodness to tell me your name?"

The radiance was all about her and she was part of it. Aquero stood at fingertip distance, her arms crossed over her breasts, her face full of sorrow. Then very slowly she let her arms drop down, holding them a little way from her sides with palms turned outwards and fingers spread as if she sought to gather up the whole world. Still slowly she raised her arms again, her fingers together like the two halves of a shell just above the blue girdle at her waist. She had not moved her head but she was looking upwards and the roof of the cave was swirling, primeval mist through which there flowed an unimaginable power. Her voice, speaking in patois, was old and young, birth and death combined like white pearls on a link of eternity.

"Que soy era Immaculada Counceptiou."

The cave was empty of all light save the flickering candles and the first streaks of dawn. Bernadette stood up, rubbing her eyes a little. Her Aunt Basile was shaking her slightly, her voice testy.

"Did Aquero tell you her name? Is it as we thought?"

"I must go to L'Abbé Peyramale," the girl said.

Her brow was slightly furrowed and she was muttering under her breath. She was still muttering when she turned in at the presbytery gate, and the little knot of relatives stayed in the road, chattering together in low voices as they shielded themselves with shawls and capes from the pelting rain.

"Yes, what is it?" L'Abbé Peyramale looked up irritably as the tap on his study door disturbed the half-hour meditation he allowed himself every dawn.

"Father, Aquero has told me her name," Bernadette said, adding a hasty curtsey.

"And?"

"She didn't say anything at first and I went on asking her and then she said 'I am the Immaculate Conteptiouna——' something like that. I think that's right because I've been saying it under my breath all the way here."

"Say it again!" he demanded.

"I am the Immaculate Conceptiouna," Bernadette repeated.

"Immaculate Conception? Is that what you heard?"

"Yes, Father, but I can't say it properly."

"Do you know what it means?"

She shook her head.

"But the words, 'immaculate conception'—have you heard them before?"

"I might have done," she said, rubbing her nose, "but I can't remember."

"You've made a mistake," he said abruptly. "Aquero must have said something else."

"No, Father. That was what she said."

L'Abbé Peyramale rose from his chair and paced the

room. When he turned to her again his voice was gentle, coaxing.

"Bernadette, do you know what a conception is?"

"No, Father."

"A conception is what happens when a male and a female come together to produce a child."

"Like mating on a farm," she said brightly.

"That's perfectly right," he encouraged. "A conception is an event, and the child born of that event is the result of the event. Nobody can say 'I am a conception'."

"Aquero said she was an immaculate contepchiona," Bernadette said helpfully.

"My dear child, only one human being has been conceived without sin, that is to say immaculate," he said patiently. "Apart from Our Lord Himself, Who was conceived in a different manner, only His Holy Mother was born without sin or stain of inherited tendency to sin. Now *she* could justly claim to be the fruit of an immaculate conception, but she could not claim to be the conception itself! First causes are implicit only in the Godhead Itself. Do you follow me?"

"No, Father," said Bernadette.

"How could you, when I can't even follow myself?" he asked ruefully. "Your lady made a mistake, that's all."

"Oh, no," Bernadette assured him. "She knew who she was."

"Then *you* made a mistake!"

"No, Father." She gave him a tranquil smile. "I didn't make any mistake."

"She must have said, 'I am the *Lady* of the Immaculate Conception."

"No, Father. She didn't say that."

"But how can you be so certain?" he demanded.

"Because I was there," she said simply. "May I go now?

Maman will be waiting."

"Yes, yes, Run along." But he spoke absently, his eyes brooding.

When the door had closed behind her he went over to the window and watched the small figure stump down the drive. There was, he thought, something indomitable in her measured tread, and for an instant he had a half-humorous vision of those clumsy wooden sabots marching steadily forward, trampling Church and State down.

"The girl must be lying," he muttered under his breath. But she had spoken the truth and he was aware that his defiance was crumbling. No illiterate child could have invented such a title, and the very fact that she had mispronounced it suggested that she was repeating something she had heard from someone else.

"Dominiquette!" He flung open the door and shouted for his housekeeper.

"Yes, Father!" She appeared so promptly that he strongly suspected she'd been listening at the door.

"Do *you* know what the Immaculate Conception is?" he demanded.

"Is that what Aquero called herself? Does that mean that she is the Blessed Virgin?"

"I don't know what it means," he said irritably. "What does the term convey to you?"

She pondered a moment, then shrugged her plump shoulders. "It's a name, I suppose."

"It's nothing of the sort," he snapped. "It's the statement of a condition and it means——"

"Means what, Father?"

"It's a knotty theological point. I'll have to write to the Bishop for advice."

"Will His Lordship know the answer?" she enquired.

"I can't tell. In fact, Dominiquette, I can't tell anything

any more," he said ruefully.

"But you believe the little girl now?"

"I cannot afford to give an opinion," he said brusquely, "but I'm troubled. I don't mind admitting to you that I'm troubled. The girl is sincere, I'll swear, but more than that I can't say."

"You should look at her eyes, Father," his housekeeper said. "Look at the little girl's eyes and your questions will all be answered."

Bernadette, rubbing her eyes sleepily as she trudged home through the rain, answered the questions fired at her by the crowding relatives as briefly as was polite. She was desperately tired and her chest was hurting. It would be marvellous to be alone for a while, to sink in memory back into the love that had enfolded her when she stood within the crystal.

"Good-morning, ladies." The calm, faintly disapproving voice of L'Abbé Pomian halted them.

"Father, we've been to Massabielle!" Aunt Lucile said breathlessly.

"Oh." His round, pleasant face hardened a little. He had been favourably impressed by Bernadette's first eager account of the little young lady she had seen at Massabielle, but since then he had regretted his own enthusiasm. The enquiries he had made concerning the family had not re-inforced his original opinion. The Soubirous parents were feckless and the girl was not even very pious. She had, he considered, been put up to the whole business, probably by one of her aunts.

It was one of these aunts, the one who kept a tavern, who now urged Bernadette forward.

"Tell Father what Aquero said," she ordered.

The girl gazed at him stolidly, rain darkening her white hood, her eyelashes beaded with it.

"Well?" He controlled his impatience and spoke encouragingly.

The child raised her arms, parting the cloak, and folding them across the shawled bodice beneath. There was something infinitely ancient in the gesture that startled him for a moment. Then, with the same grave, slow grace, she lowered her arms, holding them with outspread palms a little way from her sides before she brought her palms together again and looked up. Her voice, rich and deep for a child, echoed in the cobbled, rain-splashed street.

"I am the Immaculate Conceptiona." She had pronounced the word wrongly, but for an instant there glowed on the round peasant face a beauty he had never seen but had always known existed somewhere in the universe.

"You had best go home," he said hoarsely. "I have other business."

They curtsied respectfully, their eyes shrewd under the knotted shawls. It was as if they were mocking him for his superior education that already cut him off from the simple faith of his childhood. Only the child's eyes did not mock. They regarded him questioningly, hopefully.

"You had best go home," he repeated and went past them, hurrying.

"He believes it," said Aunt Basile, throwing her arms about her and kissing her heartily. "Soon they will all believe it!"

As if a spell had been broken they crowded about her, kissing her over and over, joined by neighbours who came running from nearby houses to find out what had happened. She was passed from one embrace to the next while the rain fell more and more heavily.

"We must get back. We'll see you later at Mass." Louise asserted herself at last, firmly anchoring her daughter's hand under her elbow and tugging at her.

In the cachot the fire had burned up and the soup bubbled merrily. Louise dipped out a cup of it and gave it to Bernadette, who had hung up her wet capulet and was rubbing her face with a small towel.

"How do you feel?" she asked timidly, remembering the strange look of exhaltation, the grave pattern of moving hands that seemed to hold close, to offer and then to pray.

"Fed up with being kissed," Bernadette said gloomily and drank her soup with relish.

EIGHT

The Prefect and the Bishop of Tarbes eyed each other like fencing opponents across the polished floor of Monsignor Laurence's study.

"The Minister of Public Worship writes that the affair at Massabielle is a danger to true religion and must be stopped," Baron Massy said abruptly.

"I have read his letter," the Bishop said coolly.

"That is why I'm here, my Lord Bishop. If you consider these revelations to be supernatural then you must speak out, or at least order a commission of enquiry."

"Tush! It's far too early for that." The Bishop waved a slender hand.

"My Lord, it is two and a half months since the so-called vision announced her title. Since then thousands of people have poured into the town to drink at the spring and pray in the grotto."

"No harm in prayer," Monsignor Laurence said mildly.

"Others come to mock," Baron Massy interrupted. "For the past six weeks there has been an epidemic of visionaries at Massabielle. Oh, I grant you the place attracts the hysterics and the sensation seekers, but a number of very devout people have had the most alarming experiences there. One young woman saw the entire Holy Family, clad in rich brocade and posturing. A child went into convulsions after seeing a golden lady with scarlet nails and black clouds enveloping her feet. And numerous well-attested reports are reaching me daily of shrieks and groans and weird music being heard there and coming from no physical cause."

"The caves are very ancient," the Bishop said thoughtfully. "I would be inclined to think that the emotions and prayers of those who go have stirred up other forces that have been dormant for centuries. When we touch invisible worlds we touch many aspects of the unknown. Given time these devilish visions, for lack of a better word, will subside, and the truth will remain."

"Then you believe in the reality of the appearances?"

"I speak in theoretical terms," Monsignor Laurence said coldly. "I have no opinion to offer on these events. The Church is not yet involved."

"My Lord!" Baron Massy expostulated. "The cave resembles a chapel already, with a makeshift altar set up, candles burning, rosaries hung up, whole families on their knees praying or washing themselves in the water, others throwing hysterical fits or going into ecstasies. I don't mention the individual dressed in white with a top hat who declares he is the reincarnation of John the Baptist and has already thrown two police constables in the river."

"What of the Soubirous girl?"

"She returned to the grotto a fortnight after the vision announced herself as the Immaculate Conception and was in ecstasy there for over an hour. There is talk of her having held a candle in such a manner that its flames licked her hand for above a quarter of an hour without any apparent pain or scorching of the flesh, but there was talk of that having occurred during a previous ecstasy."

"And since her last visit?" the Bishop persisted. "Does she claim to see or hear other visions?"

"She hasn't been near the caves," Baron Massy said reluctantly. "Her behaviour is most puzzling, most disturbing."

"In what way?"

"She doesn't take the slightest interest in what's going

on," the Prefect said. "She goes to school every day, though I understand she's very backward for her age. She answers questions about the visions in a brief, matter-of-fact way. She shows no interest in the reputed cures that are taking place, and she takes very little notice of the crowds who follow her about. I have questioned her myself and all I get is the same story. I asked her why she didn't go to Massabielle and she said she didn't feel like it, but she'd return if the lady called her. Three specialists came down from Paris to examine her thoroughly for signs of mania."

"And what happened?"

"They decided she was suffering from asthma and advised her to skip regularly for exercise," the Baron said wryly. "They did think she might be suffering from hallucinations, and the Minister of the Interior considered that phrase might be used as a lever to get her into a private sanatorium for analysis and treatment. I'm afraid your parish priest put a stop to that. He declared they'd take the child to an asylum over his dead body."

"L'Abbé Peyramale has a quick temper," the Bishop murmured, covering his mouth with his long, pale hand.

"There's not even any proof of fraud," Baron Massy said. "She will take neither food nor presents. Her parents are exactly the same. These peasants can be very obstinate, you know."

The Bishop, who was himself of peasant stock, nodded gravely.

"So, my Lord, it is up to you," the Prefect finished.

"Time solves everything," the other said calmly. "The Church cannot forbid people from praying, you know. No clergy have visited Massabielle or pronounced any opinion on what has happened. My own view is that we should defer action until the present wave of hysteria has died down."

"The Mayor, Lacade, is of the opinion that the caves

should be boarded up and samples of the water sent for further chemical analysis," said Baron Massy.

"That's entirely up to the Civil Authorities," Monsignor Laurence said.

"The Church would not prevent the closing of the grotto?"

"Dear me, no! As I said before the Church is really not involved save as an observer," the Bishop said genially. "Naturally, if there was any question of the Soubirous girl being forcibly committed to an asylum her priest has a duty to protect her, but apart from that we have no jurisdiction. Anyway, I understand she's due to make her first Holy Communion in a day or so, and I imagine that Holy Communion is not administered to maniacs."

In the sacristy of the church, L'Abbé Peyramale frowned down at the small figure before him; Bernadette was in the white communion dress that Aunt Bernarde had made for her. With its high neck and long, puffed sleeves it was the prettiest garment she'd ever owned, and her cousin, Jeanne, had lent a pair of white shoes and her own veil of blond lace.

"You are certain that you have no serious sin upon your conscience?" he was asking.

"No, Father, I don't think so."

"You have told some extraordinary stories these past four months," he reminded her sternly. "This is your last opportunity to withdraw them. If you wished to tell me privately it was—a joke, a practical joke that got out of hand, I would absolve you here and now so that you might make your communion with the other girls, and what you said to me would remain ever after under the seal of the confessional unless you gave me permission to speak out. Now, what do you say?"

"I'd like to oblige, Father," she said earnestly, "but the lady did come and it all took place as I said."

"Very well, child. Go and take your place with the others."

L'Abbé Peyramale sighed as he watched her go out. To L'Abbé Pomian who had just entered he said abruptly, "Well? Give me your opinion."

"On Bernadette Soubirous? She is one of the most earnest pupils in my communion class, and she knows less about the subject than any of them," the curate said. "She still can't even remember her catechism without prompting, and her knowledge of French is very limited."

"She is devout though?"

"She's a good girl," Abbé Pomian said slowly. "Eager to please and well-behaved in church, but one could say that of a hundred others."

"That is exactly it!" L'Abbé Peyramale exclaimed. "One would have imagined that a girl so favoured by Heaven might have shown some increase in sanctity or intelligence beyond the normal. I am troubled, very troubled."

"The girl is very truthful," L'Abbé Pomian said.

"I know. Truthful, simple and eager to improve herself, but I keep thinking that there must be something there that we've missed. I wish Heaven would grant me a sign, to help me make up my mind. We will offer a silent prayer for guidance before we go into church."

The church itself was lit only by the radiance of candles for the summer sunshine couldn't penetrate the thick grey stone with its narrow arched windows. The building was packed this morning, bright crinolines and straw bonnets striking an occasional note of colour among the sombre blacks and browns of the townsfolk. The first communicants in their white dresses and veils were faceless under their neatly banded hair, their gloved hands folded over the white ribboned prayer books that had been presented to them by the Sisters. In the background the choir began to chant the

'Asperges'.

Moving from the altar rail where the white-clad girls knelt after receiving their first wafers of unleavened bread, L'Abbé Peyramale glanced back.

He had, as usual, become so wrapped in the mystery of the ritual he offered that the Soubirous girl had gone out of his mind. Now he spotted her, kneeling at the end of the row, her eyes lowered, her hands clasped.

The girls were rising and filing back to their places. For a moment L'Abbé Peyramale thought someone had lit another score of candles, but the light came from Bernadette herself. Her small frame was outlined in a clear golden glow that swept up around her head in a crown of brilliant flame.

L'Abbé Pomian, in common with everybody else, seemed to have noticed nothing, nudged his superior under cover of his voluminous cape and lifted his brows in faint question. The service continued without interruption and when L'Abbé Peyramale looked for Bernadette as he dismissed the congregation she was no longer distinguishable among her companions.

Louise slipped away as soon as she could. There was to be a breakfast of sugared croissants, fruit and coffee for the children over at the school, so Bernadette and Toinette would be late. She was not going to clean at Madame Millet's today, but intended to set the cachot in order. So many people came in and out all day since the visions had begun that she never seemed to have a moment to herself, any more.

As she turned the mattresses briskly, beating the dust out of them with the short stick she kept for the purpose, she wondered if they might risk moving home again. Two basement rooms near the church were being offered at rock bottom rent. The rooms were dry, with skylights that let in plenty of air, and they were clean. With both François and herself in regular employment it would be possible to pay the rent for a few months, and by then somebody would surely have offered her husband the management of a mill.

Privation had steadied them both, she considered. She seldom needed to blur reality with an extra glass of red wine these days and, with strangers tramping in and out, François had little chance of lying abed.

The room clean, she took off her apron, combed her hair back into its bun, and went off to her neighbour's house.

Dr Douzous was just emerging, his lips clamped as tightly as his bag, but she risked stopping him to enquire how little Justin Buohohorts was faring.

"The child can't last more than a few hours," he said curtly. "It's a miracle he's lasted as long as he has."

"Poor Croisine! It's her last child. She lost all the others."

"Malnutrition resulting in rickets and tuberculosis," Dr Douzous said. "The poor breed like flies in these stinking hovels. The women are no sooner confined than they fall pregnant again, and their milk is meagre. These children need meat and fresh vegetables. They get sour dregs of wine and maize gruel! They need stout shoes and warm clothes, and they get damp, rat-infested lodgings in which to grow up—except that they don't grow up! They remain stunted and rickety, unless they're fortunate enough to die."

He spoke vehemently, his face red with temper. Louise understood however that he was angry not with any particular person, but with the conditions that made Croisine's children die before their time.

"You'd better go to her," he said, nodding at her brusquely. "If she only knew it it's a blessing. The child would be an invalid all his life if he survived this attack."

He strode off, still angry at the world and she tapped at the door and went into the Buohohorts' lodging. The room was crowded with neighbours, some weeping, some chattering, but the harsh, rattling breath of the baby in the cradle drowned all other sounds.

Croisine sat by the cradle, her face turned to the baby, her hands clenched in her lap.

"She has been like that all day," one of the women said in a low voice. "L'Abbé Serras was here earlier to give the Last Rites, but she didn't seem to notice."

"Fifteen convulsions," another said with a kind of melancholy pride. "I never saw a child have so many fits in so short a space of time! He's in a coma now, poor little soul."

"His breathing is weaker," another neighbour said. "Louise, you have some nursing skill. Is there anything you can do?"

Louise shook her head. The blue lips, the emaciated little face, the rattling breath told a tale that could only have one end.

"The child is dead," Ursule Nicole whispered. The rattling breath had ceased and the others held their own breaths, listening.

"I can't feel a pulse," Louise whispered back, her fingers on the limp wrist.

She was thrust aside violently as Croisine sprang from her chair and snatched up her baby.

"Croisine, you can do nothing!" Louise cried. "Let the little one die in peace!"

She spoke to empty air for Croisine, the baby in her arms, had flung open the door and was racing down the street.

"Mother of God, but she's lost her mind!" Ursule sobbed.

They still streamed after her but she was bounding along the cobbles, her hair streaming out, Justin clutched tightly to her.

"She is going to Massabielle," somebody shouted.

Louise, her own heart pounding in her ears, thought, 'Dear God, that place again! Are we never to be free of it?'

There were crowds there as usual, many of them in travelling clothes, others, evidently journalists, making notes. The cave itself was crowded with half-burnt candles, hanging rosaries, and two statues of the Virgin. In front of the niche a young gypsy girl knelt in imitation of Bernadette, her hands piously clasped, her face sparkling with mischief.

Croisine Buohohorts was struggling through the crowds round the deep pool into which the spring flowed. For an instant she hesitated as her neighbours expostulated, scrambling towards her over the rough ground. Then she plunged the baby into the icy water, leaving above the surface only the lolling head.

The gypsy's antics were forgotten as people crowded about the pool, their voices raised in argument and protest.

"The woman's run mad!"

"If the child wasn't dead before it will be now!"

"Somebody fetch a policeman!"

The voices died away uncertainly, for the small face above the level of the icy water was turning bright pink and from the open mouth came a loud yell of childish anger and bewilderment. Justin struggled violently, arms and legs flailing, his crying stronger.

The wildness died out of Croisine's face and she rose, lifting the dripping child, wrapping him tightly in her shawl.

"He will have a long and healthy life now," she said calmly, and began to make her way back up the steep path.

Louise stared down into the water. It wasn't muddy as it had been when Bernadette first scraped it out but gushed now clear and bright, splashing into the deep pool. It had gushed out of the bowels of the earth, and it was her own daughter who, obeying the instructions of Aquero, had caused it to flow.

Through her mind sped brief scenes from the past. Her brother-in-law, holding a wriggling baby in his arms and saying, "This Bernadette of yours screams as if she had ten thousands devils in her." Bernadette, lugging Toinette after her, as they trotted across the field towards her, and one of her companions saying to her, "Your Bernadette's a good little thing, isn't she?" The dark cachot with her daughter gasping for air against the barred window while François grumbled out of an interrupted sleep, "She must take after your side as far as health goes."

'She takes after nobody,' Louise thought, with a sick, lost feeling. 'She is herself alone, and she doesn't belong to me any more. She isn't my Bernadette. She's everybody's Bernadette, but most of all she belongs to Aquero.'

She turned away from the cave and plodded home across the fields, careless of the water that lapped her ankles.

The street was packed with people. She could see the tall figure of Dr Douzous as he struggled through the crowd and heard his deep voice boom out above the chattering.

"No, I can't explain it! The child is sleeping soundly with no trace of disease. He'll sleep long and wake hungry if you go back to your homes in peace."

Someone asked him a question that Louise didn't catch, but she understood the tenor of it when he roared back, "Yes, damn it! You can use the word 'miracle'. That little girl sees something down at Massabielle and if the Mother of God cures dying children then what she sees is the Mother of God—and you can quote me on that if you like!"

The crowds were surging in another direction. Louise was pressed against the wall as they swept past her, but she heard their cries.

"She's coming. Our little saint is coming!"

Bernadette, her capulet over the new white dress, was coming up the street, flanked by soldiers from the fort. She seemed at ease, her head bent, her new prayer book held tightly in her hand. All about her the shouts grew louder and several people began to clap heartily.

"Touch my rosary, Bernadette!" someone begged.

"I'm sorry, but Father won't let me do that," Bernadette was saying.

"The Buohohorts child has been cured! Thanks to you."

"I've never cured anybody," she said indifferently.

"Will you kiss my child? She's never walked in her life."

"I'll kiss her, but you'd do better to take her to a hospital, madame."

"Was the blessed Virgin very beautiful?"

"More beautiful than anyone I ever saw."

They were reaching out to snatch at her clothing, to pull at her hair. The soldiers pushed aside groping hands and hustled her through the narrow space they'd forced for her to the door of the cachot.

The door slammed shut and Louise was carried along in the wake of the crowd as they pounded on it. She raised her own voice unavailingly.

"I'm her mother! Let me pass!" But these were strangers come into the town to seek wonders, and not the neighbours among whom she had lived all her life. They had never known Bernadette when she was little trotting across the fields, with Toinette stumbling behind.

Louise stood aside, waiting for the soldiers to move the people away so that she could get back to her home. The sun had come out but she felt as if she would never be warm again.

NINE

"And that," said Inspector Jacomet, giving a final tap with his hammer, "will put a stop to it!"

He stepped back and regarded the high wooden palings that shut off the caves of Massabielle from view. Above the palings the notice proclaimed in heavy black characters the orders of Baron Massy.

"Do you believe it will?" Bernard Estrade enquired, cocking an eyebrow. "I seem to remember that when you confiscated all the rosaries and the candles the good ladies of Lourdes promptly claimed them and carted them all back again."

"This order comes directly from the Minister of the Interior," Jacomet said.

A few quarrymen were standing at the edge of the stream, their faces hostile. Jacomet glanced at them frowningly and turned again to Estrade.

"If anyone tries to enter the caves now they can be summoned for trespass," he reminded them.

One of the workmen had drawn nearer, beret in hand, his feet planted firmly apart.

"That notice!" He jerked his head towards it. "I don't read so well, but that seems clear enough. Am I right?"

"By order of the Mayor, acting by direct order of the Prefect under the jurisdiction of the Minister of the Interior, the cave of Massabielle is now closed to the public. The water is to be further analysed and if necessary sold for medical purposes."

"That's not private land," the man said stolidly. "We'll

have to think about that."

"All you need to think about," said Jacomet dryly, "is how you're going to pay the fine if you're caught trespassing."

"They'll have a lot to say about that, if it ever happens," Estrade murmured.

"They can't ignore an official notice," Jacomet said confidently.

A week later he sat in his office thumping the handsome desk of inlaid walnut until the inkwell rattled. His face, tanned and handsome under luxuriant sideburns and moustache, was beetroot with temper.

"Three times!" he exploded. "Three times those barricades have been set up and three times they've been torn down, in direct defiance of the orders of the Prefect. I have made enquiries, but of course nobody has seen anything or heard anything."

"Of course not," L'Abbé Peyramale agreed genially.

"As parish priest it is your duty to prevent such disorder!"

"Civil disorder is within your province," Peyramale said. "I'll certainly warn my flock that riot is not encouraged by the Church, but if you don't know who pulls down the barricades I'm sure you can't expect me to find out. I can only suggest you write to Baron Massy for instructions."

"I was going to suggest that you wrote to the Bishop, Father. These people will defy the law, but they will not ignore a direct order from the Bishop."

"Unfortunately His Lordship is not inclined to co-operate with the Prefect," Peyramale said. "Baron Massy has begun to erect stables on a piece of land where the canons of Tarbes were formerly buried. His Lordship considers the Prefect, by acting thus, has committed an act of trespass, and possibly of sacrilege as the old burying ground has never been deconsecrated. I fear a law suit is pending."

"As if there wasn't enough for me to worry about!" Jacomet exclaimed. "The entire district seems to have gone completely insane! I shall have to post a twenty-four-hour guard on the place as soon as new barricades are erected! I hope I can rely on you, Father, to warn your people that attacking wooden planks may seem like a joke to them, but attacking a police officer is a most serious offence?"

"You may certainly rely on me to do that," Peyramale said.

The next morning Constable Callet took up his position outside the newly-erected barricades. He was as nearly unhappy as his nature would permit. Bernadette Soubirous, he considered, was a good, pious girl to whom the Blessed Virgin herself had appeared. Now his superior had ordered him to keep people away from the holy cave. Callet had a family to consider and the dignity of his position to uphold, but he was also a good Catholic with no wish to insult the Mother of God. Glancing around he reassured himself that nobody was in sight and then, taking out his rosary, bowed his head in prayer. Fifteen minutes later, his sword on his hip, he stood with arms akimbo, watching the first trickle of people coming across the meadow.

"It's a farce!" Jacomet said angrily. "So many go to Massabielle that half of them keep Callet talking while the others pull out a plank and squeeze through a gap in order to get at the water there."

"So what can be done to stop it?" the mayor asked wearily.

"Callet has orders to take the names of all those who trespass and bring them to me," Jacomet said. "They are fined the regulation five francs at the Justice's Court."

"Which has been set up to deal with more than three hundred cases a week!" Lacade exclaimed. "They crowd the court with their knitting, and gossip and joke while sentence is being passed. Those who can't pay the five francs have it paid for them by their wealthier neighbours."

"And the water?"

"Is ordinary drinking water," Lacade said. "The analysts were unanimous."

"Then why keep up the barricades?" Estrade wanted to know.

"The Prefect will not act until the Minister of the Interior withdraws his instructions, and the Minister won't do that with a lawsuit pending between the Prefect and the Bishop of Tarbes," Jacomet said.

"Does anyone know what the Soubirous girl is doing?" somebody asked.

"They've moved from the cachot and taken a couple of rooms near the church," Estrade said. "The child goes to school every day and the church at the appointed times. She's taken up skipping to help her asthma, and she's learning how to knit. The crowds still follow her but she is not the least spoilt by all the attention."

"We don't need a reference," Lacade growled. "Do any of them go to Massabielle?"

Jacomet shook his head.

"They simply carry on their normal lives as far as they can, considering the way in which they are all questioned and followed," Estrade added.

"The girl's obstinate," Jacomet said. "Very obstinate."

The obstinate girl was at that moment hurrying across the meadows with Aunt Basile at her heels. She had been in the church waiting to take her turn in the confessional when the deep inward calling she had not felt for nearly three months filled her.

"You won't be able to get near the grotto," her aunt was lamenting. "The whole place is boarded up."

Bernadette, without answering, urged her on, tugging at her aunt's sleeve as they hurried through the flower-starred grass. It was near evening and the sun made long shadows across the river. Sun, shadows, grass and rippling water spun together in the dance of creation. And there were no more barriers of time or space. There was only Aquero filling the universe with her smile and the only perfume came from the roses on her feet.

An hour of earth time passed. The girl knelt still, unmoving, unblinking, her face reflecting what she saw as a crystal reflects the sun. A knot of women had gathered about Aunt Basile and were watching, but she was conscious only of the girl whose radiance engulfed her, drawing her soul out of her body.

She never knew when the vision went, for as Aquero faded from view her perfume and her radiant smile seemed to linger on the air, so that Bernadette had been kneeling for a little while before she became aware that she was back in the meadow with the river running between her and the boarded grotto.

"Was it the Holy Virgin?" Aunt Basile whispered. "What did she say?"

"She said nothing," Bernadette said, rising and dusting down her skirt. "She looked at me and I looked at Her."

She had turned and was walking back, her head bent. After a few moments she paused and raised her face, searching the sky with her dark eyes. Very quietly she said, "I will never see Her in this life again."

"And she said nothing more?" L'Abbé Peyramale demanded.

"She did not even say that," Bernadette explained earnestly, "but I felt the truth of her going."

"And there were no further prophecies, no messages?"

"No, Father. The Lady Vision has gone now."

"And left a pretty kettle of fish behind her," the priest muttered. "The grotto is boarded up and the people forbidden to trespass there, and those who don't consider you're a saint consider you're a lunatic or a fraud."

"I'm not any of those," she said simply. "I'm just me, Father."

"And what is 'me' going to do now?" he enquired.

"Monsieur Estrade and his sister have offered to take maman and me to Cauterets for a week," she said. "The spa water is good for asthma, Dr Douzous says, and maman has never had a holiday in her life."

"Why not ask for some of the water from Massabielle," he suggested, "Callet has a good heart and would give you a little."

"Oh, that water isn't meant for me," she said promptly. "The Blessed Virgin intends me to suffer."

"Now that's morbid thinking!" he scolded. "The Holy Mother of God loves us and doesn't expect us to inflict suffering upon ourselves."

"She doesn't expect us to avoid it either," Bernadette said, "and for me there has to be a great deal of pain."

"In Heaven's name, why?" Peyramale exclaimed.

"Perhaps she thinks I need it," Bernadette said with a sudden gurgle of laughter.

"They tell me you won't accept presents," he said casually.

"It wouldn't be right," she said.

"But a religious object?" he questioned. "You place me in a quandary, child, for the Bishop of Soissons has sent me a gift for you. A very handsome rosary."

He snapped open a velvet lined box and displayed the string of white pearls linked in gold with a magnificent cross of turquoises at the pendant end.

"For me? Father, it's beautiful."

"Certainly for you." He watched her bright face with

E

pleasure.

"It's too grand for me," she said regretfully, putting her hands behind her back.

"The Bishop of Soissons is an old man," Peyramale said. "His feelings would be deeply hurt if you were to refuse."

"But I can't take it," she said, delight turning to distress. "I'd only lose it, or be teased by the others for showing off, and Lady Vision said I was not to become rich."

"Would it please Her if you hurt a kind and saintly old man?"

"You'll have to send it back, Father," she said at last. "Do tell him how happy and grateful I am for his kindness, and ask him if, to lessen the disappointment, he would accept my rosary instead."

"Child, that's the rosary you used in the presence of the Vision!" he exclaimed. "You surely can't bear to part with it."

"Oh, I can get another one," she said promptly, "and I daresay it will please the Bishop to have it. Will you send them both back for me?"

"Yes, yes, I'll do that." He stared down at the cheap black string laid across the pearls and turquoises.

"May I go now, Father?" she was enquiring.

"Yes, yes. Run along." He went on staring at the rosaries.

At Massabielle Constable Callet shifted his position and wondered when his relief would come. His new boots were a trifle tight and his wife had promised a lobster stew for supper. Now and then he glanced towards the high boards, and once or twice he crossed himself furtively. One never knew if the Blessed Virgin would be there or not.

A carriage was bowling along the cliff road. He stood back and stared up at it, hand on his sword hilt, his hat smartly cocked.

A lady, her purple crinoline billowing about her, was

making her way cautiously down the steep path. Behind her, holding their straw bonnets, scrambled two younger girls.

"Madame, I regret that the grotto is closed to the public," he said uncomfortably.

"So I have heard." She had a Parisian accent and under the brim of her wide hat her face was dark and clever. "There is a gap in the boards though and room for people to pass through."

"I am here to arrest them if they do so, Madame," he said.

"But will you draw that fearsome sword and cut off my head if I do pass through?"

"I've no orders to do that, Madame!" he said.

"Then if you will stand aside, officer." She smiled, and beckoning her companions rustled to the gap.

The spring threw crystals up in the air and the rose-bush that clung beneath the niche bloomed with fragrant white blossoms.

The lady knelt, bowing her head respectfully. Callet walked up and down outside the barricade, wishing the leather of his boots would soften, that his relief would arrive so he could get home to his wife's lobster stew.

The lady and her companion emerged, carrying a gold-topped flask which she had evidently just filled from the pool, and a spray of the rose-bush.

"If you'll excuse me, Madame," Callet said, "it's my duty to take your name down, so that you can be summoned to appear at the Judicial Court."

"Why, certainly." She drew herself up slightly, her voice clear. "I am Madame Bruat."

"Occupation, Madame?"

"Governess to the children of the Imperial Court of France," she told him.

His jaw sagged slightly.

"The Empress believes in the reality of the Appearances," Madame Bruat said. "She may even come herself when her public engagements permit, and then you may have the privilege of taking down Her Majesty's name."

She smiled, inclining her head graciously, and with the two girls behind her, made her way back to the carriage. Through the trees he could see the sun flash on the crested door.

"And that," said Monsieur Dutour, "is that! We cannot possibly bring charges against the Imperial Governess."

"Not to mention the fact that she is the wife of an Admiral," said Lacade.

"If you don't prosecute Madame Bruat," Estrade said with a hint of malice, "you really cannot afford to prosecute anybody. If you do, you will be regarded as a tyrant by the local people."

"Jacomet has applied for a transfer to Arles," Dutour said.

"There will be several applications for transfers before the year is out," Lacade said glumly.

"I am writing to the Minister of the Interior tonight," Lacade said. "I feel it should be a formal request, countersigned by us all, asking that His Imperial Majesty be consulted. If we can no longer arrest those who trespass at Massabielle I see no reason why the barricades should remain up, or why Callet should kick his heels there all day."

The others considered and nodded gravely.

"So we write to the Emperor!" Lacade banged his hand upon the table and said, with sudden vehemence, "Gentlemen, do you realize that six months ago none of us had even heard of Bernadette Soubirous, and now her name is in every newspaper in France? For myself I find that extraordinary!"

In the Bishop's Palace the Bishops of Soissons and Tarbes conferred together, a decanter of brandy between them. On the table at Monsignor Laurence's elbow lay the two rosaries entwined in the velvet-lined box.

"The gift touched me deeply, very deeply," the Bishop of Soissons said. "To think that Our Lady gazed at that rosary!"

"My dear friend, you go too fast," the other said. "We have no idea who or what the vision was that the child claimed to see."

"Officially, no! But unofficially?"

"I cannot afford to act other than officially," Monsignor Laurence said coldly.

"But you must admit the possibility——"

"I admit every possibility. The girl is pious and adolescent and may very well have been hallucinating. She may be a clever little actress who wished to draw attention to herself. Her family may be accepting secret gifts of money which they intend to spend later. The girl may even have been the dupe of the Evil One. In this modern world it is not fashionable to speak much of the power of evil, but you and I know that disbelief in the Devil is his most potent weapon."

"But we cannot stand aside for ever, my Lord," the older Bishop argued. "The Emperor himself has now given orders that the barricades be removed."

"And nobody is having any more visions."

"Which does not stop the crowds who flock there in ever-increasing numbers, or the reports of miraculous cures."

"Rumours, and rumours can be exaggerated."

"Then it is our bounden duty to investigate them."

"It is our duty," said Monsignor Laurence severely, "not to lose our heads. I am not denying the possibility of visions, but I am insisting that we proceed with the utmost caution."

"You agree then to investigate the happenings at

Lourdes?" The old man leaned forward eagerly.

"No, no, I shall not be personally involved in any enquiry," the Bishop of Tarbes said. "What I am considering is the setting up of a Commission of Investigation, composed of clerics and laymen with a strong contingent of doctors."

"You will give the final verdict?"

"I will pronounce on the findings of the Commission, but if my findings are positive, then the whole matter will have to be submitted to the Holy Father in Rome."

"Will you interview the child?"

Monsignor Laurence shook his head. "I will not even look at a picture of her," he said firmly, "and I will not travel to Lourdes. No, I will appoint the Commission and leave its members to do the necessary work."

"The Emperor has pronounced himself a firm believer."

"Tush! The Emperor is influenced in such matters by the Empress, who is an extremely superstitious lady. I take no heed of the Emperor!"

"But you will set up a Commission?"

"I will do that," Monsignor Laurence agreed, "as I have been requested to do so by a brother bishop."

"And when may we expect a verdict? I am no longer a young man."

"It will be the New Year before I will have convened the Commission," Monsignor Laurence said thoughtfully. "The members of the committee will themselves require investigation by a sub-committee before they can be regarded as bona-fide. Every cure will have to be closely investigated. and natural recovery ruled out as beyond the bounds of possibility. The girl will have to be cross-examined as will all the witnesses. Oh, at a rough guess, I'd say we can hope to receive the evidence and opinions of the committee within three or four years."

"The child so obviously believes in what she saw," the Bishop of Soissons said. "I wonder how she will feel when she learns there is to be an ecclesiastical enquiry into every aspect of her life."

"My dear fellow," Monsignor Laurence said, "if Bernadette Soubirous is what I believe her to be the prospect will not cause her the slightest anxiety."

TEN

The Bishop of Nevers leaned back comfortably and read again the closing paragraphs of Monsignor Laurence's episcopal statement.

"In the Holy Name of God, guiding ourselves by the rules wisely laid down by Benedict XIV in his work on the Beatification and Canonization of Saints for the separation of false and true visions;

"Having regard to the written evidence of medical men whom we have consulted in connection with the numerous cures obtained as a result of the use of the water of the Grotto;

"And having invoked the light of the Holy Spirit and the assistance of the Blessed Virgin, we declare as follows:

"Article One—We believe that the Immaculate Mary, Mother of God, truly appeared to Bernadette Soubirous on February 11, 1858, and on subsequent days to the number of eighteen times in the Grotto of Massabielle near the town of Lourdes; that these Appearances have all the character of truth and that the Faithful have every reason to believe in them with complete confidence.

"We humbly submit our own judgement to that of the Sovereign Pontiff, who is charged with the government of the Universal Church."

There was more, much more, of it. In the eighteen months since the Bishop of Tarbes had delivered his verdict on the findings of the Commission, the Bishop of Nevers had read the massive file of documents over and over again.

Now he was bound for the Hospice of the Sisters of Charity at Lourdes, and on a mission that would, he thought, be a delicate one. A private letter from Monsignor Laurence was in his wallet.

"In the five and a half years since the Appearances the girl, Bernadette Soubirous, has continued in poor health, and her family remain in the most straitened circumstances. In November 1861, as Your Lordship knows, she was accepted as a boarder in the Hospice at Lourdes and, in the two years since her beginning to lodge there, has made some progress in her education. However, the girl is now nearly twenty years' of age and obviously cannot remain at school for ever. As Superior of the Mother House at Nevers your advice and assistance would be of the greatest value."

'Which all means,' thought Monsignor Forcade, folding the letter and slipping it back into his wallet, 'that nobody knows what to do with the poor girl.'

He leaned forward, gazing through the window with interest as the horses began the slow pull up the steep drive to the Hospice. A file of white pinafored pupils went past, their eyes swivelling in the direction of the carriage. On the front steps, another child sat, swinging her legs. As the vehicle was drawn to a halt and the Bishop emerged, she sprang up and began to pull at the bell-rope hanging over the front door with more energy than skill.

"Enough! Enough! You'll deafen the neighbourhood!" he exclaimed. "I'm here to see the Mother Superior. Will you find one of the Sisters for me?"

One of them was at that moment fluttering out, waving away the child, kneeling to kiss the Bishop's ring and exclaiming, "My Lord Bishop! We didn't expect you so soon! Do pray come in. Reverend Mother Alexandrine is prepared for you, my Lord, or if she is not she will be the very moment she knows that you are here."

"Then why not tell her?" he suggested gently, and followed at a more leisurely pace as she scurried ahead.

"My Lord Bishop!" Reverend Mother knelt to greet him, her fine dark eyes eager. "This is a great honour! Did you have a pleasant journey?"

"Slower than I expected due to the press of people along the roads, Mother Alexandrine."

"Ah! the town is always crowded now! You'll take some refreshment?"

"You're very kind," he said, glancing with appreciation at the daintily appointed table.

"And all those at the Mother House at Nevers—Reverend Mother General, in particular? Are they all quite well?"

"Quite well, and send their love and greetings."

"But you are not here to speak of that, my Lord, are you?"

"No, I am here to speak of Bernadette Soubirous," he confirmed.

"The child has been with us these past two years. We have given her a small room of her own, and Sister Victorine has been given charge of her education."

"How has that progressed?" he asked with interest.

"She has learned to speak French quite prettily," Mother Alexandrine said slowly. "She has also learned to read and write, though her spelling is wildly inaccurate. She can sew and cook a little, but beyond that she has only one talent."

"And what is that?"

"Goodness," said the Reverend Mother simply. "She is good, my Lord. I have never known any soul nearer to God, and that troubles me."

"In what way?" he enquired.

"She has been most highly favoured by the Blessed Virgin Herself. Hell is jealous of the citizens of Heaven, and the Devil sets snares for the pure in heart. So far Bernadette has fallen into none of them, but we cannot protect her for ever. Already she is displaying signs of worldliness."

"In what way?"

"She shows an interest in fashion," Mother Alexandrine said. "Sister Victorine had caught her letting out a skirt and inserting a crinoline frame, and only last week I found her curling her hair and tying it up with a very gaudy red ribbon!"

"Surely that's only natural in a normal young woman."

"Bernadette is a chosen soul and cannot be allowed to be natural," she said flatly. "She must be guarded against the stain and corruption of the world, my Lord."

"Yes, of course. Poor soul!" The Bishop chewed a bit of meat and said briskly, "Then let us go and see this pure soul. I'd like to catch her unawares."

"She will be in the kitchens at this hour. If you will follow me?"

He dabbed his lips with a napkin and rose.

The big, stone-flagged kitchen was warm and steamy. In a low chair by the fire, industriously scraping carrots, was the child who had rung the bell so vigorously.

"Bernadette, this is Monsignor Forcade, Bishop of Nevers," Reverend Mother began.

"But we've already met!" he exclaimed. "No, no, don't get up! If Reverend Mother will excuse us, I'll just pull up a chair, and Bernadette and I will have our little talk here."

"Certainly, my Lord." She set another chair and glided away.

The Bishop narrowed his eyes and stared at the girl opposite him. She was, he thought, exceedingly small and thin, so that it was no wonder he had mistaken her for a child. Her face was round and pale, the mouth too large with a sensual fullness of the lower lip that disturbed him. Her curly hair was tied back under a striped kerchief and she wore a dark dress under the white pinafore. Her eyes, regarding him as steadily as he regarded her, were enormous, peat brown and long lashed.

"So you are Bernadette?" he said at last.

"Yes, my Lord."

"And how is your health? I understand you were so sick last year that the Last Rites were administered to you."

"I had asthma so badly that my lungs were inflamed, but I was much better later."

"You drink the waters of the Grotto?"

"Many times, as Holy Vision bade me."

"And now that the Holy See has approved the visions, your enemies are vanquished."

"Enemies?" She looked at him in surprise.

"Baron Massy has died; Inspector Jacomet and Monsieur Dutour have been transferred."

"They were not enemies," she said. "They were only doing their job."

"But they were harsh on their questioning of you."

"As to that." She gave him a suddenly mischievous smile. "As to that, my memory is very bad!"

"And now you live here, with the good Sisters."

"I see my family every day," she said.

"Are they well?"

She nodded, looking pleased.

"My father is working regularly," she said, "but my mother is with child again. The doctor says that everything is going well, so we must trust in God and not worry."

"How many of you are there now?"

"My sister Toinette is seventeen. She is courting a good man, a miller. Jean is twelve and will be going out to work soon. Justin——" Her face clouded a trifle. "Justin is not well, but there seems to be nothing the doctors can do. I have another brother now. Bernard is four years old and very healthy. We are hoping this new baby will be a girl."

"So you are very fond of your family," he observed.

"Yes, my Lord."

"And have you no thought of starting a family of your own? You say your sister is courting. Will you perhaps be considering marriage?"

She was silent.

"An attractive young girl like you must have admirers," he pressed. "You must have wondered sometimes how it would be to have a husband. The love of a good man is a great blessing."

"I know, but it wouldn't be enough for me," she said, hesitatingly. "I would always be seeking something more, something a human love couldn't give me."

"But if you won't wish to marry, what are you going to do with your life?" he asked.

"I thought I would work as a maid for somebody," she suggested.

"And be interrupted ten times a day by people questioning you about the visions?"

"They question me here too," she interrupted.

"But the Sisters can give you some measure of protection," he explained. "If you go back into the world you'll not have a moment's peace. The crowds will flock around you every day."

"As if I were an animal in the zoo," she agreed, with a tinge of bitterness.

"Had you thought of a religious vocation?" he enquired.

"That's not possible," she said quickly. "I've not much education and I've no dowry."

"An exception might be made. The Sisters of Charity of Nevers could be persuaded to admit you as a postulant."

"I don't think I want to be a nun," she said, looking alarmed. "I'd have to leave Lourdes and my family, wouldn't

I? And never see Massabielle again? I go there nearly every day to pray, and I couldn't give it up. I don't believe I've any calling to the religious life."

"This isn't something to be decided in a moment," he cautioned. "You must pray about it, ask for guidance."

"And if I were to become a nun," she added, "I'd not want to be a Sister of Charity. I'd rather be a Sister of St Vincent de Paul. They have such pretty headdresses, and then they have their Mother House in Paris. I'd love to visit Paris and see all the grand buildings and the soldiers on parade."

"You are still very young," the Bishop said wryly.

"Then couldn't matters be left as they are? she pleaded. "I'm very happy here, and I can see my family and my friends whenever I choose."

"There's no hurry." He rose, motioning her to remain seated. "But think about it, and in a year or two you may have reached a different decision."

In the parlour Mother Alexandrine regarded him anxiously.

"Well, my Lord?"

"Not well," he said briefly. "The girl has no vocation for the religious life, and she is too attached to her family, even to the Grotto itself. Certainly she hasn't cultivated detachment."

"But the girl herself? Am I not right in calling her a chosen soul?"

"Oh, undoubtedly! But the chosen must be guided and protected," the Bishop reminded her. "The Mother House at Nevers would be willing to take her as a postulant if she gave her consent. Naturally there must be no compulsion. The girl is free to make up her own mind. Above all she must not be given to understand that the Sisters of Nevers are eager to have her as a postulant. We don't wish to encourage her to think of herself as anybody special."

"No, indeed, my Lord Bishop," she agreed earnestly. "But she is special, isn't she?"

"A rough diamond," he said, "but with the grace of Heaven, Reverend Mother, we will chisel out a saint!"

Bernadette had finished scraping the carrots and was washing her hands. Her fingers were bare of rings. She gazed at them, trying to imagine a wedding ring on the third one. It was the duty of a woman to marry if she could and to bear children, but she had never seen the man for whom her heart had missed the slightest beat. Her mother had often said how happily married she was, but Bernadette had seen her crying with no bread in the house and the chilblains broken and bleeding on her knuckles. There had been other moments too, times when she had lain in the darkness of the cachot, listening to the smothered sounds that came from the mattress where her parents entwined. She had accepted such facts of life but she didn't crave the experience of them for herself.

Drying her hands she thought wistfully that it would be nice to have a ring without having to have a husband too. Of course if she entered the religious life then she would wear a wedding ring as the bride of Christ.

'And a fine bride for Him I'd make,' she thought in amusement. 'I have no talent and no dowry, and no inclination to it either.'

She hung up the towel, took off her pinafore and reached for her capulet. She would slip away now to see how her mother was and to pay her respects at the Grotto.

The Soubirous family lived now at a small mill not many paces from the old Boly mill. Her father rented the place and so far was doing good business. It was odd, the girl thought, how before Lady Vision had appeared nobody wanted to do business with her father, and now people flocked to buy his flour.

She found her mother sewing flounces for a dress. Toinette was going to a dance with her suitor and had a hankering for frills. Bernadette held the dress up, admiring its pink flounces.

"Toinette is going to look lovely, maman," she said. "Are you happy about this match?"

"He's a good steady man. And you, child? Is it true that a bishop came to see you today. L'Abbé Pene was passing and happened to notice."

"When wasn't L'Abbé Pene passing and just happened to notice! But a bishop did come today, to see Reverend Mother, and he was good enough to talk to me."

"Will they never be done with their questions?" Louise wondered.

"Oh, this was about my future." Bernadette laid the dress across the foot of the bed and sat on the stool next to her mother. "They don't know what to do with me, you see. I have no religious vocation, and I'm not minded to marry, and there's not much else I can do. If I become a maid I'll have to keep breaking off my work to answer questions, and an employer isn't going to like that very much."

"There is always a home for you here," Louise said.

"I know that, but with the new baby coming and Justin not so well, I'd keep everybody awake at night with my stupid coughing. Anyway, there's no hurry to decide, the Bishop says. After all I can always go back to Bartres and help with the sheep."

"They are saying that when you stayed at Bartres you built shrines up on the hills and taught the lambs to kneel down when you recited the Creed."

"Do they really say that?" She laughed in delight. "Have you ever tried to make a lamb do what it doesn't want to do? And I couldn't even say the Creed properly in those days! Poor Madame Laguis had a hard time getting anything into my thick head."

"It seems such a long time ago when we talk about it," Louise said thoughtfully. "But you're not yet twenty, still at the beginning of your life. I sometimes feel as if everything is slipping away from me, and, I want to hold onto it before it's gone for ever."

"That's nonsense, maman! Nothing we have known can be lost," Bernadette said briskly. "And I have to go too! I hope Toinette and Baloume have a good time at the dance —Baloume is going too, isn't she?"

"With her own young man," Louise nodded. "She's turning out better than I thought she would, that girl."

"I'll see you tomorrow," Bernadette promised.

It was almost twilight as she set off along the forest road, but a steady trickle of people still wound its way between the trees. The Bishop of Tarbes had sent word that three chapels were to be built above the Grotto, and the Grotto itself was to be consecrated and an altar erected there. Already a statue had been put up in the niche and another one commissioned. Bernadette hoped the new statue would look a little more like Vision Lady. The one that stood there now had a sugary expression that made her want to giggle. The meadows were to be drained too, and the course of the Gave changed, to make it easier for pilgrims to come. There would be an esplanade lined with statues of Carrera marble, and the main basilica would have a cross of beaten gold on its dome. It all sounded very splendid, Bernadette decided, and a long way from the chapel for which her Aquero had asked.

But the cave was unchanged. She drank some of the water from the brimming pool and then knelt to tell her beads, a small figure unnoticed among all the other girls in their white capulets, the visitors in their bright crinolines with their top-hatted escorts, the frock-coated doctors with their patients, the priests talking quietly among themselves. She had forgotten them all before she had recited a decade of her rosary and was back in memory with the smiling, gracious young girl who had blazed brighter than the flaming crystal in which she stood.

"Excuse me." The strange gentleman had to repeat himself before she looked up and rose.

"Yes, sir?" She curtsied politely.

"Is this really the place where the Blessed Virgin appeared?" the man was asking.

"Yes, sir. This is the place."

"I would like to visit the child's home," the gentleman said. "Not to intrude, you understand. I don't wish to intrude, but I'd deem it a privilege to meet some of the family."

"They live at a mill near the old Boly mill," she said. "Anyone in town will tell you where they live."

"The girl herself is at a convent, isn't she?"

"Yes, sir."

They had turned and were strolling along together.

"Did you know that the girl was dumb and never spoke at all until she went to the Grotto?" he said.

"No, I didn't know that," she said with interest.

"Oh, it's been hushed up, I believe, to save the family from embarrassment," he said.

"Is it really? I didn't know that, either," she said.

"But the girl does give interviews now," he was saying. "I believe it's necessary to make an appointment, and if my work brings me to this part of the world again I'll do what I can to catch sight of her. Are you from Lourdes?"

"Yes, sir."

"You must count yourself fortunate to be able to visit the Grotto every day if you choose."

"Oh, yes, sir!"

"But you may even know the Soubirous girl!" he exclaimed. "Do you know her?"

"Yes, yes, I know her."

The gentleman was shaking her hand fervently.

"A privilege! A rare privilege," he was saying, "to meet somebody who actually knows the visionary! Can you give me some idea of what she's like?"

"Oh, she's very ordinary," Bernadette said. "She's nothing much to speak of, sir."

She dropped a quick curtsey and went ahead of him, snuggling more deeply into her capulet for the September breeze was cool, and her chest was beginning to hurt again.

ELEVEN

"It's time to leave, Bernadette." The Mother Superior spoke quietly, wondering if the girl was asleep, for she sat with her head on her arm and her eyes closed.

"I'm quite ready, Mother Alexandrine," Bernadette's voice was clear and steady in the gloom.

"It's almost three-o-clock. Did you sleep?"

"Very well, indeed." Bernadette sounded faintly surprised at herself.

"And everything is packed?"

"Yes, Reverend Mother." She indicated the canvas bag in which her possessions had been stowed. Two linen night-gowns and bedcaps, two chemises, three pairs of drawers, three flannel petticoats, six pairs of woollen stockings, a dark blue dressing-gown and a pair of slippers, a bag containing her toilet articles. She herself wore a dark blue dress and cloak, and had tied a striped kerchief over her hair. In her pocket was the rosary that L'Abbe Peyramale had given her to replace the rosary she'd given to the bishop, and round her neck there hung on a leather cord the silver medal of the Virgin that the family had given her as a parting present.

"It has taken you a long time to make up your mind to take this step," Mother Alexandrine could not resist saying. "I cannot help wondering what finally decided you."

"Because I have been so happy here," the girl said simply. "I was giving up nothing by staying with you, and that seemed wrong to me."

"You have become very dear to us all," Mother Alexandrine said. "If at any time you wish to return to us, remember that the door is open."

"Yes, Reverend Mother." She took a final look around the narrow whitewashed room and went quickly down the stairs to where Leontine, the other intending postulant, waited in the dark hall.

The small coach, the Bishop's crest upon the door, set off down the steep drive.

"We are going to stop at Massabielle," Reverend Mother said. "You will wish to say a prayer there before we take leave of your family."

"You're very kind, Mother Alexandrine," Bernadette said.

Her heart had begun to beat painfully fast. Now that she was leaving Lourdes for ever, it was possible that the Vision would return, albeit briefly, to wish her farewell.

Dawn was silvering the tips of the Pyrenees as they reached the Grotto, but the cave itself was dim. In the niche the white statue gleamed faintly. Above the cliff many of the trees had been felled and a little further to the left was the chapel. It had been consecrated by the Bishop of Tarbes and she had attended the service dressed in a flowing white robe. The crowds had streamed after her, calling upon her to bless them and heal them, and in the end she had been smuggled back to the Hospice and an armed guard set about the walls.

This morning the spring gushed even more strongly, splashing down the deep channel into the pool. There were plans to enclose the spring and pipe its water into a series of stone baths where the sick and the dying could be immersed. Further chapels were to be built and a Calvary erected higher up the mountain. The railway would come directly to the town and already several hotels were being built on the surrounding hills.

But the Grotto itself would remain almost as it had been on that February morning eight years before when she had gone out to gather wood with Toinette and Baloume.

Her eyes searched the niche fervently, willing the Lady to come back for a few moments only. The niche remained dark, the white statue motionless and smiling a sugary sweet smile that had in it nothing of the gaiety or power of the living reality she had witnessed.

The niche remained dark and cold. Mother Alexandrine touched her on the shoulder and spoke gently.

"Bernadette, we have to go now. We have many miles to go before night and your family still wait to say goodbye."

"Two minutes more! Just two minutes." She spoke urgently, her eyes still fixed on the niche.

"Child, we have to go now! Please to get up," Mother Alexandrine said firmly. The girl, she saw with alarm, was starting to cry.

"The Grotto—I'll never see it again," Bernadette was sobbing.

"The Grotto is not your private domain and our Blessed Lady is everywhere," Mother Alexandrine said. "Hurry into the carriage and wipe your eyes. You don't want people to see you've been crying, do you?"

"No, Reverend Mother." She blew her nose obediently, took one last miserable look at the empty niche and trailed back to the coach.

Her family were clustered at the front door of the mill. She looked at them, shawled and capped, their feet planted firmly on the cobbles, and was struck by sudden pity. They had never wanted any fame or riches, only a decent livelihood and a roof over their heads. That, at least, they now had, and not one of them had accepted gifts or bribes, but fame they had not been able to avoid and it sat uneasily upon their broad peasant shoulders.

"Papa." She reached up to kiss him, but he looked stiff and ill-at-ease, twisting his old beret round and round in his hands.

Toinette, plump and emotional, had flung her arms about her.

"You'll not forget me?" she was enquiring earnestly. "You'll not forget I was with you on that first day at Massabielle?"

"No, indeed! You and Baloume!"

"I was wondering." Toinette hesitated and then rushed on. "I was wondering if you'd mind if I changed my name to Marie, in honour of the Vision. I know I never saw anything but I must have been very close to Her at times!"

"So near you could have touched Her," Bernadette said. "I think it would please Her greatly if you were to call yourself Marie."

Her brothers stepped forward to say goodbye, looking as solemn as if they were at a funeral. Justin had died the previous year, but Jean, at fifteen, now worked full-time with his father in the mill, and Bernard was seven and had started school. Apart from Justin and the two babies who had died when Bernadette was small, two more Soubirous children lay in the cemetery beyond the church, Jeanmarie, who had lived less than two years shared a grave with his baby sister who had been born the previous year and had lived for barely a day.

"Maman?" She glanced at Louise who had already lost five of her nine children and was now losing her sixth.

"I have soup ready," Louise said, evading her daughter's embrace. "There is nothing like a mug of good, hot onion soup to set one up for a long journey!"

She was bustling round with trays on which mugs of the fragrantly steaming liquid reposed. The soup was thick with bits of white bread and generously laced with red wine.

Bernadette drank and was glad that its heat gave tears the excuse to come into her eyes. Cold morning air and emotion combined, making her so dizzy that she staggered a little.

"Now be sure to wrap up warmly!" Louise was ordering. "Do as the good Sisters tell you, and remember to take your medicine, and write to me. L'Abbé Peyramale has promised to read your letters to us all."

As if a spell had been broken the others were crowding around, kissing her, patting her on the back. Through the gathering light the bulky figure of L'Abbé Peyramale loomed up, his voice genially teasing.

"Have you any further orders for the clergy before you leave?"

She shook her head, trying to smile, recalling with a kind of wonder how frightened of him she had once been.

"We must leave now," Reverend Mother was saying. "Bernadette? Leontine?"

Under her watchful eye they resettled themselves in the coach. Through the window as she poked out her head Bernadette could see her mother standing at the back of the small crowd. Louise was holding the tray of empty soup-mugs, and she was smiling with her head up and her eyes proud. Across the intervening space mother and daughter looked wordlessly at each other. Then the carriage began to move and the shouts of farewell grew fainter as they bowled along the Tarbes road.

"If I were you," said Mother Alexandrine, addressing the roof of the coach, "I'd settle down and have a good cry."

The two intending postulants looked at her, glanced at each other, and burst into a concerted storm of weeping.

Traces of tears still marred their faces when shortly before ten that night they were carried swiftly along the winding road towards the high gates of the Convent of St Gildard.

Below them sprawled the streets and houses and market squares of the town of Nevers, and the town itself nestled amid luxuriant green meadows and fields of waving corn like a jewel on green velvet.

Above the gates, rimmed in gold under the rising moon, the words, "God Alone," stood out against the purpling summer sky.

A squat figure in a dark cloak was unlocking the gates. The horses moved slowly through, and the iron clanged shut.

In the lamp-lit parlour a small group of senior nuns waited. The Mother General, Mother Josephine, was completing her brief lecture.

"We are entrusted with the care of an innocent and holy soul, and you are aware that our responsibility is a heavy one. Make no mistake, my daughters! Even here, within these walls, the Evil One will seek to snatch this treasure of Heaven for his own fiendish Kingdom, and he will employ subtle means. We must be constantly on our guard, for if we fail in our duty, we all bear the blame. I think I hear the bell. We will seat ourselves and await the newcomers."

She herself sat behind the flat-topped desk where she spent much of her day writing reports, her strongly-marked features impassable. At her side Mother Marie Therese, Mistress of Novices, stood, her beautiful hands clasped within the wide sleeves of her black habit, her face a perfect cameo within the white-edged coif.

A tap sounded on the door. "Enter." Mother Josephine's harsh voice was raised commandingly.

She was very small and looked much younger than her years. They had seen photographs of her, but they had not expected her to look so defenceless. She had obviously been crying and now and then she gave a small sniff.

"So you are the new postulant. You arrive so late that we have to delay the Grand Silence because of you." Mother

Josephine looked her over critically and added, "Not a very promising start, is it?"

"I'm very sorry, Reverend Mother," Bernadette said, flushing deeply.

"But you had a good journey? You look as if you've been crying."

"Nearly all the way here," she admitted.

"Excellent. Tears are the sign of a true vocation," Mother Josephine said. "I am always very wary of too much enthusiasm. Now we must take your name and age."

"Bernadette Soubirous. I was twenty-two in January." She looked at them in a puzzled fashion, wondering why they pretended not to know.

"And what value do you think you can be to us here?" Mother Josephine was enquiring.

"I don't know, Mother."

"The Order of the Sisters of Charity of Nevers is a strict Order," the Mother General said. "Our gates are locked, not to keep the nuns in, but to keep the world out."

"The novices and Sisters here come from all over France," said the tall, beautiful nun who stood at the side of the Mother General. "Many of them are descended from ancient and distinguished families. Others have special talents which they place at the disposal of the Community. Many of our nuns embroider or design illuminated manuscripts. Others are skilled herbalists and work in our infirmary here. Other Sisters have gone into the mission fields or have become teachers in our Daughter houses. Reverend Mother and I wonder what skills you can offer."

"But I really can't do anything," Bernadette said in distress. "I can read and write better than I could, and I can speak French without too many mistakes, but I can't do anything else at all. I did tell the Bishop I wasn't much use at anything when he came to see me in Lourdes."

"What were you doing when the Bishop came to

Lourdes?"

"I was in the kitchen." She frowned, trying to remember, for there had been so many visits from so many bishops. "I think I was scraping carrots."

"We could put her to work in the kitchens," Mother Josephine said.

"She doesn't look very strong to me," Mother Marie-Therese said.

"Mother Victorine will tell you my health is better than it was," Bernadette said eagerly. "I do have attacks of asthma and my lungs were weakened by my last illness, but I take medicine regularly and am really quite fit these days."

"And rather too immersed in the state of her own health," said Mother Marie-Therese in a low voice. "It might benefit our new postulant to see those who are truly sick and never grumble about it."

The Mother General nodded. "You will make yourself useful in the kitchens," she said, "and you will spend some of your time cleaning the sluices in the infirmary. Many of the patients are advanced cancer cases and bear their suffering with a dignity and fortitude that will serve as an inspiration to you."

"Mother Marie Therese is our Mistress of Novices," she continued after a moment. "You will be entirely in her charge, and if you require anything or are in trouble, she is the person who will help you."

"Our Rule here is simple," the Novice Mistress said. " 'God Alone' is written over the main gates and engraved upon our hearts and minds. We desire nothing but God, and to obtain our desire we give up everything we possess. We detach ourselves from everything and everybody in the world."

"Yes, Mother."

"You've brought with you the required undergarments and nightwear?"

"In my bag, Mother."

"Tomorrow morning you will be given a postulant's dress and coif, and the things you have on will be donated to the poor. When you are admitted into the Community you will receive the ring, veil and habit worn by the professed Sisters. You will not be required to make your Final Profession until you are absolutely certain of your vocation. Do you follow that?"

"Some of it, Mother. I feel confused at the moment," Bernadette said.

"There remains the question of your name," Mother Josephine said. "Those who enter here discard their earthly names and take others. You will wish to choose the names of Marie Bernarde."

"Yes, indeed I would." Her face glowed with pleasure.

"And now we must speak of the visions of Our Blessed Lady which you claim to have had, and which the Church has declared as genuine," said the Mother General.

"Even here, in this Convent, some ripple of interest has been caused. For that reason I would be pleased to hear an account of the events from your own lips, and for that reason I have assembled the rest of the community together so they may have the pleasure of hearing it too."

She had risen and was leading the way out of the parlour down a narrow echoing corridor which opened out into a vaulted hall. On the long, carved benches were ranged the Sisters in their black and white austerity, while the postulants sat on the floor, their brown coifs and dresses giving them the aspect of fallen October leaves.

"Sisters, this is Sister Marie Bernarde, who is joining us as a postulant," the Mother General said. "She has agreed to relate to us the story of the visions with which she was favoured. When she has finished the matter will be closed and will not be referred to again."

She motioned Bernadette to the raised platform and sat

down in the high-backed chair.

Every eye was upon her, every head inclined in her direction.

"Please continue, Sister Marie Bernarde," the Mistress of Novices continued.

"When I was fourteen I went out to gather wood at a cave called Massabielle," Bernadette began nervously. "In the cave I saw a little young lady dressed in white with a blue girdle and a yellow rose on each foot. She had a rosary over her arm of pearls and gold, and she was more beautiful than anyone I ever saw. I saw her again seventeen times more. She spoke to me in patois, and sometimes she smiled and laughed, and sometimes she wept."

"Tell the Sisters what she said to you," Mother Josephine invited.

"She said many things," Bernadette said. "I heard her voice in my forehead and in my heart. She gave me a prayer and three secrets that are only for me. She said I wouldn't have a long life, and that I'd be happy in the next world but not in this one. She told me to pray for sinners."

"Tell the Sisters about the finding of the spring," said Mother Marie Therese.

"Oh, yes." She felt tired and hungry, and her head ached. "The Lady said, 'Go drink and wash yourself at the spring.' I thought she meant the Gave, but she pointed inside the cave, and I went there and scraped up a puddle. I didn't want to drink it."

"That argues a want of humility that I find very shocking," the Mistress of Novices said.

"It was filthy dirty!" Bernadette exclaimed indignantly. "You wouldn't have fancied it yourself!"

Mother Josephine coughed silently.

"But the spring ran clear, did it not?" she said.

"Oh, yes. Later on it ran clear and made a big pool. Oh, and the Lady told me to eat the herb growing by the spring.

F

There were no herbs there, but there was some grass, so I ate that."

"Tell us all about the day that Our Blessed Lady announced Her title," said the Mother General.

Bernadette hesitated. For eight long years she had repeated those graceful ritual gestures and that simple sentence over and over again until they had lost all meaning. Now, her legs aching from the long hours jolting in the carriage, she stared back at the row of pale faces in their coifs. How could she possibly convey to these cloistered women the reality of that cold, damp morning and of the blazing crystal that had enshrined her, lifting her out of her human condition?

She moved her hands in the ageless gestures and heard her own voice vibrate with remembered glory.

"I am the Immaculate Conception." There was a long silence. Then Mother Josephine rose.

"We are grateful for Sister Marie Bernarde's description," she said. "The matter is now closed, though we are at liberty to ponder it in our hearts. We enter now the Grand Silence, but our two new postulants are absolved for tonight, so they may bid farewell to Mother Alexandrine and partake of a little light supper after their journey. Remember, my daughters, God Alone this night and all nights."

Mother Alexandrine was embracing them, and Leontine was crying again. The other nuns were gliding away like black and white ghosts into the vastness of the convent. Bernadette was so tired that the scene blurred before her eyes.

"Come along, Sisters, and we'll give you something to eat now."

Mother Marie Therese was smiling at them. She looked so beautiful and so holy that Bernadette felt even smaller and clumsier than usual as she followed her.

TWELVE

It's been a long year," said Monsignor Forcade.

He spoke thoughtfully, gazing into the parlour fire.

"A long and eventful one," the Reverend Mother General agreed.

"And the problem of what to do with her still remains." There was a slight tartness about Mother Marie Therese's voice.

"What is your opinion?" the Bishop asked. "You have had the most to do with her this past twelve-month."

"She has not admitted me into her confidence," the Mistress of Novices said.

"But she is obedient and devout surely?" Monsignor Forcade said.

"Obedience and devotion are not enough," she said. "One expects to find in a visionary some extraordinary quality of holiness, but I must confess that I find nothing remarkable in Sister Marie Bernarde. Her intelligence is limited and she is still addicted to worldliness. I found her only yesterday actually waltzing up and down the cloister! It sets the young postulants a very bad example."

"She is still young and very gay," Mother Josephine excused.

"Gaiety has no place in the religious life," Mother Marie Therese said severely. "We choose immolation that we may make reparation for the sins of the world. We choose to spend our days in a living crucifixion. Sister Marie Bernarde is forever joking. I've even heard her whistling!"

"She has a joyful heart," said Mother Josephine. "Surely you will grant her that, Mother Marie Therese."

"Sister Marie Bernarde has not favoured me with any confidences," the Mistress of Novices said.

She was remembering a recent incident that had hurt her deeply.

She had gone out into the garden down to where a statue of the Virgin looked over a deep, fern-fringed pool on which water-lilies floated. A small figure had been kneeling there, dabbling her hand in the ripples.

"Sister Marie Bernarde, you are not at Recreation with the others," Mother Marie Therese chided.

"I needed to be alone." The small figure rose, gazing down into the water still.

"You are not feeling homesick, are you?" Mother Marie Therese asked.

"Is it wrong?" Bernadette's dark eyes were troubled. "I have tried very hard to detach myself, but I do think about my family, and I would give anything in the world to visit Massabielle just once more."

"So you come here, to be alone for a while with the grass and the water and the holy statue?"

"It's a beautiful statue," Bernadette said. "There is something about it that reminds me of——"

"Of Our Lady of Massabielle?"

"I do wrong to talk about it," the girl said in a low voice.

"This statue is known as Our Lady of the Waters," the Mistress of Novices said. "And you must never feel that there is any subject barred between you and me. As Novice Mistress it is both my duty and my pleasure to receive the confidences of my postulants and novices. If you wish you may come here for part of every Recreation and nobody will disturb you."

"You're very kind, Mother," Bernadette said, but her tone

was formal and she had drawn away slightly.

"You must feel free to come to me with your problems," Mother Marie Therese persisted. "You say this statue reminds you of your vision. If you could explain exactly what you mean we could draw some interesting theological implications from it together."

She spoke warmly, her fine eyes glowing, but her companion had turned back to look into the pool again, and her tone was indifferent.

"It's impossible to explain, Mother—oh, do look at that little duck swimming among the reeds there! He has feathers tipped with black and a bright red bill!"

The Mistress of Novices had knocked upon a door and it had been closed in her face. For an instant she burned with the sting of humiliation. Then she bowed coldly and went back to the lawns where the novices were playing ball.

"Her soul has passed through experiences we cannot even begin to imagine," the Bishop said now.

"So it is believed," said Mother Marie Therese.

"Are you telling us that you don't believe it?" Mother Josephine asked.

The Mistress of Novices hesitated, then threw out her hands in a gesture of despair.

"I want to believe it!" she exclaimed. "When I heard that Bernadette Soubirous was coming here, that I was charged with her care and guidance, I was overjoyed. Now I would gaze into eyes that had seen the Holy Virgin! Now I would be permitted an intimate friendship with a chosen child of Heaven! I wouldn't be human if the prospect didn't thrill me. Oh, I knew she was an unlettered girl who'd once kept sheep, but there was an innocent simplicity in that which appealed to me greatly."

"And how do you feel now?" Monsignor Forcade asked.

"For more than a year," said Mother Marie Therese,

"I've had daily contact with Sister Marie Bernarde. I regret having to say this—I regret it bitterly—but she is commonplace. I thought it was shyness that kept her from opening her heart to me, but I believe now that there is nothing there to reveal. She is shallow and ordinary, and I cannot help asking myself if Our Blessed Lady could ever have appeared to such a girl at all. There is another postulant in my charge, Sister Angelique. She too has had visions of Our Lord Himself on Mount Carmel, and there is in her a delicacy of soul that is irresistible. A few days ago I accompanied both the young Sisters into the chapel for a period of meditation. Sister Angelique was at once plunged into silent tears before the crucifix. When we came out I asked Sister Marie Bernarde what thoughts had come to her as she gazed at Our Lord in agony, and do you know what she said? She said, 'I was thinking Our Lord needed a bit of a clean-up, so I'll slip in later and give Him a polish.' And that is the girl to whom the Queen of Heaven is said to have appeared!"

"You are very silent, Reverend Mother General," the Bishop commented.

"I was thinking of what happened just before Christmas," Mother Josephine said. "When Sister Marie Bernarde was so ill that we thought she was dying?"

"And you sent for me in the middle of the night to administer the Last Rites, and to invest her with habit and veil."

The three of them fell silent, remembering that night of rain and wind when Sister Marie Bernarde had suddenly begun coughing blood and gasping for breath. The Bishop had arrived in haste to be met by a deeply troubled Mother Josephine.

"The child wishes to be admitted as a novice into the Congregation, my Lord," she said. "She hasn't completed her term as postulant, I know, but she has set her heart on receiving the veil and ring."

"In her case an exception can be made," he had agreed.

It was an eerie scene with the candles flickering on the whitewashed walls and the voice of Mother Marie Therese below the howling of the wind that shook the windows as, on behalf of the sick postulant, she made the temporary vows of poverty, chastity and obedience that would, when she chose, be rendered final at the Immolation Ceremony.

There would be, thought the Bishop, no final vows for little Sister Marie Bernarde for it was obvious that she was dying, but at least she had the black veil and habit and the gold ring of her Profession.

But scarcely had he placed the ring on her finger when colour flooded her face and she said, her voice strengthening with every word, "I'm not going to die this time."

"Do you mean to say that we got the Bishop out of bed in the middle of the night and you're going to recover!" Mother Josephine expostulated. "If you're not dead by the morning I've a good mind to put you back among the postulants."

"I went right up to the door," Bernadette said, "but God sent me away. He said, 'It's not you I want but your maman'."

"We heard within the month that her mother had died of a heart-attack," Mother Josephine said now.

"She was always deeply fond of her family," the Bishop recalled.

"And we are still left with our problem," the Mistress of Novices reminded them. "Most of our other novices complete their training in our Daughter houses, and the fully professed are licensed for work in the mission fields and our schools and hospitals. Where can we send Sister Marie Bernarde?"

"We must keep her with us, of course," Mother Josephine said.

"And make her feel that she is privileged?" Mother Marie Therese compressed her lips. "That would be a grave mistake."

"Are the Sisters assembled?" the Bishop asked.

"And have been this past hour," the Mother General said.

"Then we will join them." He rose and paced the corridor into the vaulted hall where the Congregation waited. His eyes, scanning their ranks, were shrewd, his voice rich and deep.

"Sisters of Charity of Nevers, I am here today, as you know, to award you the licences that will enable you to take up certain kinds of work beyond the walls of this Mother house while completing your novitiate. Will Sister Marie Bernarde please step up here?"

She came eagerly, a diminutive figure in her flowing robe.

"I'm afraid we have no licence for you, Sister," Monsignor Forcade regretted. "Reverend Mother General says you're completely useless at everything."

"I told you that myself," Bernadette said indignantly, "and you said it didn't matter."

"Well, it poses a problem." He gnawed at his thumb-nail, watching her. "We have a reputation to maintain and sending you out into the world would inevitably damage it. I am hoping that Mother Josephine will have the charity to let you remain here."

"If Your Lordship so orders then I am constrained to obey," Mother Josephine said.

"Very well, then." He waved a beringed hand. "You are to remain here, Sister Marie Bernarde, and I can only advise you to try not to get under everybody's feet. You are excused from the ceremony."

For an instant her eyes blazed at him. Then she lowered

them, knelt to kiss his ring, and walked quietly from the hall.

It was chilly in the garden, but her face was scarlet. She had tried so hard to fit in the life here and still she seemed to make no progress. The Bishop had spoken so harshly that she had longed to shout back at him. 'Can't you even give me credit for doing my best?' It would, she thought darkly, serve him right if he got a stomach-ache.

"Bernadette?" The voice and face were familiar, but she couldn't place the man walking to her across the grass. He wore the soutane of a priest, and she was certain she knew him from somewhere, but there were so many priests who visited the convent.

"Don't you remember L'Abbé Aravant?" he enquired.

"My godmother's brother!" Her face lit up and she put out both hands, speaking rapidly in the patois she never used here at Nevers. "You were so kind to me at Bartres! I can remember that very well, but you've grown older!"

"And you look no different," he marvelled. "You have a child's face still, and the same eyes. I noticed your eyes long ago, before you went back to Lourdes and the Vision came."

"Have you come from Lourdes?" she asked eagerly. "How are they all there?"

"Very well, indeed. Did you know that L'Abbé Peyramale used his own savings to buy the mill where your father lives, and he has presented it to him?"

"That was a generous thought!" She clapped her hands together in delight. "Did L'Abbé Peyramale send his regards to me?"

"Many times. He is to be elevated to Monsignor."

"Ah! if I had my way I'd make him an Archbishop!" she exclaimed, laughing. "And my family? My sister, Toinette-Marie? She is with child, you know."

"And blooming," he smiled. "You would scarcely recognize Lourdes now. It's crammed with pilgrims, and not only from France. They come from all over Europe, from America too. There are photographs of the Grotto, and of you. I have them to show you."

She studied them for a long moment, a variety of expressions flitting across her face.

"The Grotto is almost unchanged," she said at last. "I can still see the place where I used to kneel."

"It is to be paved and a brass plaque laid there."

"Heavens! how grand! And this is me? Do people honestly want to look at photographs of me?"

"They buy them," he told her. "They buy statuettes of you too, and medals with your face on them. Whatever Rome may decide in the centuries to come the world already regards you as a saint."

"Good Lord! I wish somebody would tell the Bishop!" she exclaimed, amusement rippling out of her. "The poor man is so disappointed in my progress here that he doesn't know what to do with me."

"People are calling you a saint," he repeated obstinately.

"I hope not too many of them are doing that." Her laughter dying, she began to look a little anxious. "I wouldn't fancy frying away in Purgatory while they were all praying to me to intercede for them."

"But you're safe enough," he argued. "Our Lady promised you happiness in Heaven."

"Only if I keep to the straight and narrow down here," she said gloomily, "and so far I don't seem to be doing terribly well at anything."

"You're too hard on yourself," said L'Abbé Aravant.

"Not hard enough!" she exclaimed. "I cannot even carry out the normal penances because of my stupid asthma. I help in the infirmary, you know, and half the time I'd rather be lying there with the patients. That shows you what a slug-a-bed I am!"

"Is your health so bad?" he asked anxiously.

"Between you and me," she said solemnly, "I'm a bit of an old crock, Father. They tell me I'm nearly twenty-four. There are mornings when that prayer-bell goes when I feel about ninety!"

"They are saying there may be war between France and Prussia before any of us are much older," he said.

"Are you afraid of that?"

"Of war? I don't think so. I'm not very interested in politics."

"You have had no revelations?" he asked.

"Revelations about what?"

"About the war, about the world that is changing so rapidly. It's rumoured you have had further visions, that you have been visited here by Our Blessed Lady."

"It isn't true," she said sadly. "I don't like to disappoint you, Father, but nothing like that has happened. Even the visions of Massabielle are growing dimmer in my mind. I can still see Aquero, but the times She came have all run together in my memory."

"After so much glory," he marvelled, "it seems incredible that you should be forgotten in such a way."

"L'Abbé Aravant," she asked abruptly, "what do you do with a broom when you've finished sweeping the floor?"

"I put it back in the corner," he replied.

"There then! The Virgin used me as one uses a broom to do a particular job, and now She's put me back in the corner," Bernadette said simply. "I don't think brooms have any right to complain. Oh, but they're coming out and I've been gossiping here instead of taking my turn at raking up the leaves!"

She hurried off and he stared after her for a moment

before turning to greet the Bishop and the Mother General who had paused to enjoy the sunshine.

"L'Abbé Aravant? But you are surely an old friend of Sister Marie Bernarde!" Mother Josephine exclaimed.

"I knew her when she was a child," he returned.

"My sister was her foster mother for a time, and Bernadette went back later to work on the farm. I'm afraid they were a little severe with her sometimes, but she never bore a grudge."

"She's a generous soul," said Monsignor Forcade, "and she is learning to control that hot temper of hers."

"But she feels she is a disappointment to you here," the priest said.

"Would you have her self-satisfied?" Mother Josephine asked. "We are trying to knock her into shape."

"I hope you'll do it gently," he murmured.

"I think you may leave your little protégée safely in our hands," Mother Marie Therese said, a little snap in her voice.

She walked away with more than her usual dignity, her thin brows raised in an annoyance she was too well-bred to display. There were times when she grew utterly tired of the vanities of those who were supposed to have renounced the evils of the world. L'Abbé Aravant evidently considered himself privileged to have known Bernadette as a child.

The novices were walking in threes, according to the strict rule that discouraged any tendency to strong personal friendships. A group of them were playing ball. Under the trees Bernadette—a silly rustic name if ever there was one —was raking up the glowing leaves into little piles. There was, Mother Marie Therese noted with annoyance, a streak of dirt across her nose.

"Excuse me, Mother Marie-Therese." A young postulant had left her companions and was tugging gently at her sleeve.

"Yes, Sister Bernarda?"

She smiled at the fresh face turned towards her.

"I've been here two days, Mother," Sister Bernarda said timidly, "and I've not met Bernadette Soubirous yet. My parish priest assured me that she was at St Gildard. Could you point her out for me?"

The Mistress of Novices reached out and tapped Bernadette on the shoulder.

"Yes, Mother Marie Therese?" She dropped a swift curtsey and stood waiting.

"This is the visionary of Lourdes," Mother Marie Therese said.

The postulant's mouth fell open in dismay. Her voice squeaked with disbelief.

"*That* little bit of a thing!" she exclaimed.

"As you see." Bernadette rubbed her nose and favoured them both with an urchin grin. "Just a little bit of a thing, my dear. Nothing more."

'She has charm,' Mother Marie Therese thought, walking away from them. 'There is something very lovable about her. But has she truly seen and spoken with the Mother of God?'

She turned aside abruptly and entered the chapel. She was forty years old and had already lost count of the hours she had spent on her knees before the high altar with its Gothic candlesticks and great carved crucifix. She had knelt away her life, she thought now, pouring out her soul to the Most High. She fasted beyond the Rule, flavouring much of her food with wormwood. She spent much time in compiling long reports on her novices and in writing long letters to those who had left the Mother house. In her prayers she remembered them all with love and anxiety lest any of them should have fallen from the high standards in which she had trained them.

'All my life,' she thought, 'I've sought to do Your will, oh

Lord. All my life I've studied, fasted and prayed. All my life, Lord, and never caught a glimpse of that which I have worshipped. Yet to an ignorant little peasant You sent Your own Mother. Why not to me? Why not?'

THIRTEEN

"I think it's time we talked about your taking your final vows," Mother Josephine said.

"As you wish, Reverend Mother General."

"No, Sister Marie Bernarde, not as I wish, but as *you* should wish," Mother Josephine said firmly. "You have been with us for twelve years and it is time you took the final step. You know it yourself, so what keeps you from it?"

"I don't feel that I'd be of any more use to the Community as a fully professed nun than I am now."

"It is not for you to judge your own value," Mother Josephine said severely.

"Ask Mother Marie Therese," Bernadette said, with a gleam of humour. "She will tell you my lack of value."

The Mother General sighed. It was no use in pretending any longer that there was any sympathy between the Mistress of Novices and the visionary. Mother Marie Therese had made it quite clear that in her eyes Sister Marie Bernarde was a commonplace soul who may or may not have had any visions of the Holy Virgin.

"They would have a different tale to tell in Lourdes," she contented herself with saying. "A statue of St Michael has just been erected at the main entrance to the Sanctuary of Massabielle. It was donated by a cavalry regiment and is intended to symbolize the repulsion of evil from the holy place. And you have seen photographs of the crowned Madonna that stands in the square before the Basilica."

"It's all changed now," Bernadette said. "The meadows

and the Nicolau mill paved over, and the stream diverted, and statues everywhere. If I ever went back I'd likely get lost."

"There are processions too," Mother Josephine reminded her. "Tens of thousands of pilgrims walk with their candles in honour of Our Lady."

"Well, that'll please Her." Bernadette looked a little happier.

"And there are so many cures. A Medical Bureau has been set up to investigate them.

"She never said anything about cures," Bernadette said flatly. "She wanted people to pray and do penance, and she asked for a chapel not a forest of basilicas. No, Mother Josephine, Lourdes and I parted company a long time ago, and since then I've done nothing worthwhile."

"My dear child, you're talking nonsense!" Mother General exclaimed warmly. "During the war you were a tower of strength to us all. The soldiers we nursed here told me they'd never known such a calm, cheerful nurse as Sister Marie Bernarde. Modesty is one thing, but this continual self-deprecation is a different matter! You must stop thinking of your imperfections and allow yourself to remember your achievements."

"What achievements?" Bernadette demanded in astonishment. "I spend half my time lying in bed ill!"

"You have become, by dint of sheer application to duty, a competent nurse and skilled needlewoman. The Bishop was admiring your lace work only the other day."

"And I still can't spell properly or meditate with any success."

"And there you evade the issue again." Mother Josephine rapped the desk sharply. "Sister Marie Bernarde, what is it that troubles you so?"

There was a pause. Bernadette's eyes gazed beyond the

Mother General into a space beyond time, and her voice was heavy with grief.

"Have you ever been in swirling darkness?" she asked at last. "Have you ever felt as if storm clouds covered the sun, as if even the sun itself had never existed? Have you ever tried to pray and found your words made no sense and were addressed to emptiness? Have you ever felt such a complete absence of hope that death would be a blessing, except that you're afraid to die because you have no hope of salvation?"

"Have you known such moments?" Mother Josephine asked.

"I've known nothing else for twelve years," Bernadette said simply. "Year after year, Reverend Mother, with a stone weighing down my heart, groping my way through a blanket of cloud. Even the visions have grown dim and muddled. Oh, I can testify to them still, but it's as if it all happened a very long time ago to another girl."

Mother Josephine bit her lip thoughtfully. "Have you never heard of the Dark Night of the Soul?" she asked.

"The experience that saints go through before the final union? But they are saints and better able to bear it."

"We all have our dark nights," the Mother General said. "Merit lies in struggling through them. You have always concealed them under a cheerful manner. The other Sisters regard you as tranquil and serene."

"One suffers without making others miserable," Bernadette said briefly. "You know there was a time when I made up my mind to be a saint! I wrote on my private notebook, 'I must become a very great saint'. Can you imagine it! A great saint, when I cannot even pray any more or do my work properly because I'm so often sick."

"I have the physicians' report," Mother Josephine said abruptly.

"Have they found something else wrong with me?" Bernadette asked. "You know, I have a suspicion they invent diseases and try them out on me."

"They write very clearly and comprehensively," Mother Josephine said. "The asthma has seriously weakened your lungs, it seems, and there are early traces of tuberculosis apparent. They fear that your stomach is so badly ulcerated that internal bleeding has already begun. Your joints show unmistakable signs of rheumatoid arthritis and the tumour on your knee—I'm sorry, Sister, but it has been diagnosed as malignant and inoperable."

"Anything else?"

"Your wisdom teeth are impacted and the pains in your head are caused by inflammation of the sinuses."

"Good Heavens! there's not much left of me that's sound, is there?" Bernadette exclaimed, her infectious laughter rippling out. "Do they say how long I've got?"

"Less than six months. I'm deeply sorry."

"Six months more than I expected, or hoped."

"For that reason I urge you to make your Final Profession."

"You know," Bernadette said thoughtfully, "these past years, in some part of me, I've always held a door ajar in my life so that I could slip away from here, if the clouds grew too dark, and return to the Grotto. But I'll never go back there now, will I?"

"You'd never survive the journey," Mother Josephine said.

"Then there's no sense in holding open the door," Bernadette said briskly. "I'll make my Final Profession as soon as you please."

"You may find it helps you a great deal," the Mother General said encouragingly.

Bernadette, reaching for the heavy stick on which she

limped about, shook her head.

"The clouds will cover me now until my death," she said calmly.

Outside the parlour she stopped to draw breath. There were days and nights now when she could scarcely breathe, and her leg hurt so badly that she stuffed a corner of the sheet in her mouth to stop from crying out.

In the garden the cold wind launched a September attack. She lowered herself to a bench and leaned over, shuddering as blood poured from her mouth and nostrils. The attack was over sooner than usual, but it left her with pounding temples. She closed her eyes briefly, summoning the energy to move on into the chapel.

"Wasting time, Sister Marie Bernarde?" The Mistress of Novices had paused by the bench and was looking down at her critically. The years of sacrifice and penance had sharpened the older woman's features until her pale skin was stretched like paper over the elegant bones of her skull.

"I'm doing my job, Mother Marie Therese," Bernadette said.

"And what job is that, pray?"

"Being ill." She met her superior's gaze with a solemn face. "I'm beginning to think that's the one thing I can do really efficiently."

"Then, my dear child, you ought not to be out in this cold wind!" Mother Marie Therese said in concern. "What is wrong with you, today?"

"Rheumatism, asthma, ulcers, tuberculosis, cancer and impacted wisdom teeth."

Bernadette struggled to her feet and gave the startled Novice Mistress a decidedly mischievous grin. "Take no notice of me," she advised. "We invalids always exaggerate a little."

In the chapel Sister Julienne had just finished her task

of cleaning the brass and silver. She waited as Bernadette inspected the results, her face falling slightly as the other said tartly,

"Very pretty on top, Sister, but what happened to underneath the knobs?"

"Nobody can see them," Sister Julienne protested.

"God can," Bernadette said. "Do the job properly, there's a good girl. Wait! Give me a cloth and we'll tackle it together. Nothing like a bit of company on a cold day!"

"Are you well enough? Mother Eleanore told us you'd been ill."

"My child, before you've been here very much longer," Bernadette said severely, "you'll learn that the sun rises every morning, sets every evening, and that Sister Marie Bernarde has a different ailment for every day of the week. Now stop chattering and let's get on!"

But the visits to the chapel grew fewer as the winter progressed. The taking of her final vows was, in the end, no more than another ceremony in the long series of rituals that had woven a bright thread through the dark tapestry of her years in the convent.

She wrote to the remaining members of her family to tell them of this final step, but it was so long since she had seen any of them that they seemed remote, like strangers who had touched her life briefly and gone. Her father had died eight years before, confused and inarticulate to the end, and both Monsignor Laurence and Monsignor Peyramale were gone too.

But there was no shortage of bishops and priests as the new year of eighteen seventy-nine came in with heavy snows. Over and over again she repeated to the crowds of visitors the story of those days when she had gone to see and speak with Aquero. Over and over again, her voice hoarse with fatigue, while they leaned forward eagerly, anxious not to miss a word of the narrative.

"In the month of February, on the eleventh day, in the year eighteen fifty-eight I went out with my sister and a school friend to gather wood from the banks of the Gave near the caves in the great rock of Massabielle."

Baloume and Toinette, both running ahead and splashing through the icy water. She could see them so clearly and see herself bundled in the old white capulet with her wooden sabots and the cheap black rosary in her pocket.

"I was unrolling my stocking when I heard a noise like a gust of wind."

If she had not looked up at that instant of time to see the trees stretched flat against the windless sky, what direction would her life have taken?

"I saw a light with a little, young lady in the midst of it."

There was a white statue in the cleft of the rock now. It was nothing like Aquero.

"She gave me three secrets and a prayer for myself alone. She said I would be happy in Heaven but not on earth, and that I would not have a long life."

She had kept the secrets faithfully and repeated the prayer every day, but she was already thirty-five years old and Heaven was getting further and further away all the time.

"She told me to kiss the ground and pray for sinners. She directed me to a hidden spring and told me to drink the waters of it and wash in it and eat the grass there."

She could still remember that muddy water, and the bitter taste of the grass, and the people staring at her in astonished pity.

"She told me She wanted a chapel there and She wanted people to go there in procession."

That first chapel had a Basilica built on top of it now, and in the Basilica were chapels dedicated to many other saints.

The trees had been cut down along the forest road to make room for the great marble buildings, and there was talk of building yet another church to fit the tens of thousands of pilgrims. The old parish church had been pulled down and a bigger one built, with a crypt where Monsignor Peyramale was buried. There were souvenir shops, and hospitals, and hotels, and the old cachot had been cleaned up and a plaque fixed over the door.

"Sister Marie Bernarde is very tired," Mother Marie Therese was saying.

"If she could repeat the actual words of the Holy Virgin when She revealed Her title."

"Que soy era Immaculada Councepciou." She had long since lost count of the number of times she had repeated those words and gestures. They had no meaning in the darkness where she dwelt but other people found such pleasure in hearing her say them that it was a pity to disappoint them.

"The Official Commission will be here tomorrow," Mother Marie Therese said. "They require you to testify again for the Vatican Records."

"But I told it to them, over and over," she protested.

"Nevertheless, you are to submit yourself for cross-examination."

"Very well." She spoke submissively, fighting back her impatience.

"We will leave you for a while. There are about a hundred photographs of yourself to be signed and sent to various convents. Can you get them done by Vespers?"

"If I must."

"It's a question of obedience, Sister Marie Bernarde." The Mistress of Novices rose, smoothing her habit. "Are you feeling better today?"

"I feel dreadful," Bernadette said flatly.

"Remember that suffering and mortification purify the soul."

"Yes, Mother Marie Therese." Bernadette gave the brisk little nod that was characteristic of her.

"It pains me to say this," the Mistress of Novices said, "but it strikes me you are still prone to vanity. Your handwriting has developed a certain flourish. Remember that as nuns we must seek to be as sugar in water, leading the hidden life. Personal vanity has no place here."

She stopped, frowning, for Bernadette had rounded her finger and thumb into a circle, and was smiling at her impishly.

"If you are entirely without vanity yourself, my dear," she said, "put your finger through that."

Mother Marie Therese put both hands behind her back and said quellingly, "It's a pity you have never learned to take life more seriously. I will come up later to see if you are more comfortable."

"I cannot help it," she confided later to the Mother General. "I look at her and say to myself, over and over, 'Why you? Why were you chosen? And were you chosen or was it all the dream of a sick child who wanted to be important? All these years, Mother Josephine, I've watched her, and I still cannot decide."

"I cannot help you," the Mother General said. "In the end we must each of us make up our own minds."

"Of one thing I'm very certain," Mother Marie Therese said. "Sister Marie Bernarde is in very great pain. Something must be done to alleviate it."

"The physicians have suggested morphine," the Mother General said. "I have decided against it."

"Surely, in the name of charity——!" the Mistress of Novices began.

"True charity gives that which is most needed by the

recipient. Sister Marie Bernarde feels very strongly that she does not deserve the supernatural favours that have been shown to her. She would not thank you if she lived out the last few weeks of her life in a drug-induced stupor. So, no morphine!"

"As Reverend Mother General wishes," Mother Marie Therese bowed coldly.

The weeks crawled towards Easter. Propped up in a long chair, for she had begun to suffocate if she lay down, Bernadette listened to the bells ring out. She would have liked to see the chapel again with the flowers on the altar and the silver brightly shining, and the Sisters chanting together. So many good women! All her life she had been surrounded by good people, and yet the only place where she had ever felt at home was at Massabielle.

"How are you feeling?" Sister Dorothea was enquiring.

"Ground up like a grain of wheat." She managed a small joke.

"May I slip down to the chapel for a few moments?" Sister Dorothea begged.

"Yes, of course." She managed another smile as the novice left the room.

The calendar on the table said April the sixteenth. Twenty-one years to the day since she had knelt in ecstasy with a candle flame playing over her hands without scorching them. She would have given her soul for a candle now because she was icy cold and the room was growing darker. There were faces looming in the darkness, evil, grinning faces waiting to snatch her soul.

"I've set everybody such a bad example," she said aloud. "I was rude to a policeman once. He told me it was wrong to eat grass, and I snapped back that I'd noticed him eating salad and where was the difference? And once at Bartres I took the sheep into someone else's field because the sun was shining there. And I never bothered to confess it."

"Sister Marie Bernarde, in these last minutes of your earthly life, will you testify as to the reality of the Appearances at Massabielle?"

That was the Reverend Mother General. The room was filled with nuns. Some instinct must have brought them from the chapel.

"Sister Marie Bernarde, will you testify for the last time?"

"On a day in February when I was fourteen I went to gather wood at a cave known as Massabielle."

Her voice, rasping now, went on as the room grew darker. Storm clouds were rushing in and a gust of wind rattled the windows.

"Have you any last requests?" Mother Josephine was asking.

"Pray for me," she called out, her voice suddenly loud as it had been in childhood. "Pray for me, a sinner, a poor sinner——"

Her head dropped to the side as lightning split the sky, and down her cheek ran a very small tear. It gleamed like a crystal for an instant, and then the room grew so dark they could scarcely see.

EPILOGUE

1934

He was an old man and the exciting events of the previous month had wearied him, but he had promised himself this trip to Bartres. It had meant taking a couple of days off from his part-time job as a market gardener in Pau, but at seventy-seven he felt he could afford to take the occasional holiday.

He had stopped off first at Lourdes where he had enjoyed looking up old friends. Nearly all of them were dead now and others were fading from his memory, but in contrast the figures of his childhood were becoming clearer as if his life were rounding itself into a circle.

The town itself had changed over the years, modern hotels and hospitals dominating the lower hills below the high peaks. The old Savy mill and the meadows were paved over and a broad esplanade now separated the river from the rocks of Massabielle.

At the main entrance he had paused to admire the three Archangels, Gabriel, Raphael and Michael, who pointed the way past the granite Calvary to the Rosary Square. He had paused again at the railed, garland-decked statue of the Madonna whose head was raised to the gigantic cross that dominated the high hill above the Basilica. The Basilica itself with its domes and spires and mosaic floors and gold and silver chapel was, he considered, very fine. Such a riot of jewels and marble and flags of all nations made his head spin a little, and he had passed on gratefully beneath the triple arch to the great rock with its cave and the niche where roses still grew, twining about the feet of the white Madonna.

Lighting his candle and placing it carefully on the spiked stand, the old man had joined the long line of pilgrims and shuffled around the cave, touching his rosary to the damp rock. Bernadette would have been pleased to find the Grotto so unchanged. It was, he thought, a very great pity that she had not been brought home again but her body, still incorrupt after more than fifty years, was displayed at Nevers in a glass case.

Her sister and brothers were all dead now, of course, but he had enjoyed a glass of wine with her nieces and nephews at the mill which Monsignor Peyramale had bought for François Soubirous.

Now, having taken the rattling bus along the winding road, he plodded up the steep path to the sheepfold. There were a few people here too, some examining the souvenirs they had bought at the Lagues farmhouse, others adding their names to those already scratched on the half-door of the sheepfold. It was cold and fresh up here, and he sat down on the rock and watched his breath whiten the air.

"So touching, to think of the saint guarding her sheep here!" A woman in a fashionable fox-trimmed coat was speaking to him. Her French was good, but her accent marked her as Belgian.

"This was where she felt the call to return to Lourdes," he nodded.

"You are a native of the district?"

"I am Justin Buohohorts," he told her.

"Buohohorts? The name sounds—but surely you are some relation to the child cured so long ago. I was reading of it."

"I am that child," he said proudly. "My mother ran with me to Massabielle when I had been given up for dead, and plunged me into the freezing pool. I must tell you, Madame, that I was guest of honour at the canonization in Rome. I had a private audience with His Holiness and I was interviewed by the newspaper.

"And you actually knew Saint Bernadette!" She was gazing at him in awe.

"I was ten when she left Lourdes, but I remember very well."

"And what was she like?" the lady demanded eagerly. "She is being spoken of as one of the greatest saints of all times, but to have actually known her! What was she like?"

He frowned, remembering the brisk little figure in the white capulet as she went down the street towards the Grotto. His mother had told him over and over that he owed his life to Bernadette Soubirous, and he had been a little shy of her in consequence. But she had often stopped and spoken to him in a friendly, ordinary manner. She had had a rough voice and a merry smile and her eyes had always been looking through him at something else. In Rome they had called her the perfect reflection of the Holy Virgin. It was a fine description, as fine as the great Basilica and the torchlight processions and jewelled altars, but it didn't seem to have much to do with that little figure in the white capulet. It was as if the real girl eluded them. Only here at Bartres, in the cold mountain air with the snow-clad peaks dyed scarlet by the setting sun, did some echo of her sound, as faint as bells ringing from the distant valley below the cross-crowned hill.

"Bernadette?" He rolled the name over in his mouth with a sense of ownership. "Ah, Madame, she was just a little bit of a thing!"

AUTHOR'S NOTE

My thanks are due to the Sisters of Le Bon Sauveur, Holy-head, for their kindness in allowing me the use of books from their library.